# Windows

ANNI HOLLIDAY

**T**

The manufacturer's authorised representative in the EU
for product safety is Authorised Rep Compliance Ltd,
71 Lower Baggot Street, Dublin D02 P593 Ireland (www.arccompliance.com)

This is a work of fiction. Names, characters, businesses, places, events
and incidents are either the products of the author's imagination
or used in a fictitious manner. Any resemblance to actual persons,
living or dead, or actual events is purely coincidental.

Troubador Publishing Ltd
Unit E2 Airfield Business Park,
Harrison Road, Market Harborough,
Leicestershire. LE16 7UL
Tel: 0116 2792299
Email: books@troubador.co.uk
Web: www.troubador.co.uk

ISBN 978 1836283 072

British Library Cataloguing in Publication Data.
A catalogue record for this book is available from the British Library.

Printed and bound by CPI Group (UK) Ltd, Croydon, CR0 4YY
Typeset in 11pt Minion Pro by Troubador Publishing Ltd, Leicester, UK

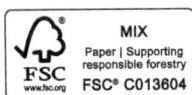

MIX
Paper | Supporting
responsible forestry
FSC® C013604

# ABOUT THE AUTHOR

Despite having written since childhood, this is Anni Holliday's first published work. She graduated in English Language and Literature at the University of Reading in 1984, completed a post graduate diploma at the Colchester Institute and pursued a career in financial services until 2023. As well as books, animals, tennis and horse-riding, she loves to travel and spent some years in the Netherlands as a teenager. She has one daughter and lives with her husband and cat in Scotland.

# 1

At the age of fifty-eight years and seven months, Ellie Coley finally had to admit to herself that she was, well, just a little bit bored. A divorcee, with her only son long-married but fiercely aware of the financial constraints and general inconveniences incurred by parenthood, she felt unneeded, frustrated and redundant. The realisation had been slow in coming. After a long career in financial services (from Martin, years back, "It's a safe bet. You'll start on a lower salary than the marketing agency you really like but you'll soon make up for it,") she'd snatched at the opportunity offered in the form of bank office closure and a large pay-off. After all, she could do all the things she'd dreamt of doing while juggling with full-time work, childcare, a husband absent too often and too long and then absent forever. She could cycle every day, do as many guilt-free jigsaw puzzles as she liked, spend time painting and visiting art galleries, read all those books she could never resist purchasing at every passing bookshop and help bring up her grandchildren.

There was the rub. The bitter, jealous disappointment of it caught her in the throat sometimes. Ellie had wanted more children, Martin hadn't. He liked his exotic holidays, expensive cars and luxury toiletries (manly ones only, of course) and didn't like his mortgage. He also liked entertaining clients on his long sojourns goodness knows where. Until one day he liked a client a little too much and didn't come back. A year later Ellie and Martin were divorced and Martin's partner was pregnant with their first of two boys. Who knows, maybe it was the divorce and its impact on Simon, or the knowledge that he had half-siblings he would never really know (Martin and Jenna having, conveniently for them, moved so far away that Simon rarely saw his father), that had determined him either to have children late in life or not at all.

Ellie learnt soon after that fateful conversation with Martin, when he'd confessed to his long-running affair and told her he was leaving, that the advised safe maximum intake of alcohol for women was two bottles of wine a week. She experimented: less than this induced a depressed insomnia; too much more and she fell into bed partly unconscious but even more depressed and with a throbbing head and rasping throat the following morning. She found the perfect remedy: the suggested safe intake plus a strong, hot toddy of whisky and water just before bedtime every day.

But today she had a double errand to run, or rather cycle. She'd ordered new LED lights for her Trek ahead of the coming winter, which were ready for collection, and she needed to find a birthday present for an overly wayward, three-year-old girl. It was the child of a distant cousin only, but Ellie was scrupulously even-handed across all infantile relatives – a fastidiousness, sadly, not truly appreciated by the recipients. Her kitchen calendar contained a confusing array of colour-coded, age-banded birthday hieroglyphics.

Ellie collected her rucksack at the back door, first checking both that her baseball cap was in it and that Alex's water bowl in the corner of the kitchen next to his food was full, picked up her gloves and stuffed them in her jacket pocket along with her house keys, let herself out of the back door, locking it behind her, and went to the garden shed where her bike was stored.

As always, after unlocking the door with the key kept in her rucksack, she stood for a moment and admired the beautiful, shiny newness of it and its sleek, uncomplicated lines. She'd saved up hard for it, even reducing her alcohol intake for a whole six months due to her old-fashioned aversion to paying in instalments for something she couldn't buy outright. That's when she'd first met Greg, who ran the bike shop in the town. She'd gone to ask his advice, with a view to buying from him, but he'd recommended, given her budget and requirements, that she buy second hand as she'd be able to get a much better model. He didn't sell second-hand bikes himself, but he had a good and reliable contact he'd used frequently before, from whom he'd receive a small commission. Ellie was surprised and impressed by his honesty and the fact he was willing to give up a sale for her benefit. She rushed to assure him that, if he did that for her, she would bring the bike only to him for maintenance and repairs.

Ellie had called her bike Porthos because of all the adventures she planned to have with it. This was the name she'd wanted to give her cat when she got him but worried about how pretentious this would sound to her neighbours when she went outside to call him home. She'd had an amazing time that summer, her first after getting the bike, initially exploring the area round her beloved home town of Linlithgow in Central Scotland, then taking Porthos on the train to go further afield. She'd cycled round lochs, along canals, on forestry tracks, along disused railway lines and, less often, through cities to visit art galleries and museums. She revelled in the independence and flexibility of travel with Porthos, never for a moment regretting the, for her, small fortune she'd spent to have him.

Ellie carefully extracted the precious machine from the shed, balanced it delicately against the wooden outside wall, picked up and put on her helmet and locked the shed door after her, carefully replacing the key in the smallest pocket of her rucksack which she then slung over her right shoulder and strapped herself into. She only just remembered to put on her gloves, so keen was she to set off on her errand.

The rush of cold air around her ears made Ellie gasp and breathe quickly, as she raced off at some speed and then gained a slower, more steady and regular rhythm, feeling her heart and lungs expand as the adrenalin fed her veins.

As Ellie cycled, she decided to visit the toy shop first.

She would chain up her bike near the cycle shop, where there were more bike racks, go to the toy shop, return to the cycle shop for her lights and then pick up her bike and go for a ride afterwards. She would need to make sure she chose a present that wasn't too big for her rucksack, or buy it today and collect tomorrow on foot. As Ellie entered the high street, she passed, without seeing, a sign attached to a lamp post emblazoning the town council's generosity in sponsoring a competition for local shop owners to demonstrate their prowess in designing and orchestrating eye-catching Christmas-themed shop window displays – "No professional help permitted."

# 2

"Bloody birds!" Billy scratched at the grey and white shit on the window with a wet paper towel as the seagulls winged a dance above, laughing squawkily at his pathetic efforts, like a group of old ladies sharing a dirty joke. He couldn't afford a window cleaner more than once a week, as ordained by the council, and was too shaky in his hands and pins to do it more often himself. Irritated but philosophical, he re-entered the shop, taking in again, with a huge sense of pride, the vast array of colourful boxes, packets and figures on the shelves and racks, representing every toddler's and young child's dreams of morphing into a farmer, zoologist, astronaut, doctor or Disney Princess. Games, puzzles and jigsaws ascended in piles from floor to ceiling, though Billy silently hoped no one would ever want anything off the top shelf unless his grandson, Andy, was doing one of his serving stints and could shimmy with ease up the increasingly rickety ladder stored in the corner. His daughter, Susan, Andy's mum, called it "the death trap" and foresaw a disaster scene awaiting some unsuspecting customer, of Billy, neck broken, lying buried beneath an avalanche of boxes and soft toys. "There are worse ways to go," Billy mouthed under his breath as he went to the bathroom at the back of the shop to wash his hands and fill up the kettle again.

As he came back through, a small shadow on the other side of the shop window glass caught his attention. He vaguely recognised the outline of a small, silver-haired, baseball-capped woman who had visited before, not that frequently but always spending a similar amount of money. She seemed to be studying the displayed wares very intently. Billy started to wonder if Andy had deliberately put something inappropriate in the window, by way of relieving the boredom he often bemoaned to his grandfather and as part of his minor sabotage plan on family life resulting from having to live it as Andy Anderson.

As Billy watched, she moved to the other window, the shop having double frontage, and scrutinised the contents there too. After what seemed an age, the bell above the door jingled and she entered the shop, carrying an already pretty full rucksack, slung over her right shoulder, from which a cycle helmet was suspended by its strap and swinging, surely uncomfortably for its owner, Billy thought.

"Good morning. Not a bad day out there. Can I help or would you just like to browse?"

The woman fidgeted as she stood, shuffling tiny feet and twisting fingers in tight, luminous, Lycra gloves.

"Good morning. Yes, I would like to browse, thank

you, but I wonder first – this is going to sound incredibly cheeky – could I make a suggestion?"

Billy was intrigued. He didn't think anyone had asked that question in the shop before.

"Of course. Is it about the opening times? I've had to reduce them, you see. My grandson helps here as much as possible, but he's got exams now and isn't able to come as often as he used to."

The peak of the cap nodded sympathetically and then immediately moved from side to side in the negative.

"I see. Yes, that's a shame for you both, I should think, but it's not that. No, it's about the window displays. They're a bit, well, a bit of a muddle, if you don't mind me saying. I think they could be much better, and that might encourage people to come in. You see, I didn't come into the shop until a long time after you opened, and it was because I wasn't tempted by what was in the window. I did eventually, because I had to, and I was really pleased I did because what you have inside is amazing."

The woman paused, slightly breathless with embarrassment after her critique and confession. She obviously knew she was blushing because she blushed some more.

Billy's first reaction was irritation. What did people think he was capable of, in here alone most of the time and not exactly in a fit state to crawl about in the small space offered by the shopfront? He opened his mouth to express these sentiments then closed it when he saw her bright, blue-grey eyes almost watering with mortification.

"Oh, right. Yes, it's hard for me. I can't really get into

the space myself anymore. My knees are bad. My grandson does the window displays, but I'm afraid he's not very imaginative and often in a rush. He prefers to chat to the customers."

She breathed a visible sigh of relief.

"Well, that's very important too. You can't be good at everything, particularly at a young age. I imagine it's important to change the displays fairly often too, to encourage existing customers to come back in? If you like, I could, well, I could have a go myself? I think I'd be able to get into the window fairly easily and, as it happens, I'm not that busy today."

Billy blinked, uncomprehendingly. Was this woman seriously suggesting that she climb into the window space and rearrange his goods? Was she bonkers or something?

"Well, I don't know about that. I mean, you're not employed by me, are you, and there's Health and Safety to consider. You could hurt yourself."

"Oh, I'm sure I'd be okay. I'm quite fit, you know. I cycle everywhere," (the helmet a pendulum again), "and I'm quite flexible. I would just be a temporary volunteer in the shop, wouldn't I? If you could maybe just help me clear out what's already there and the space in front a bit and with choosing what we put in?"

She was obviously slightly demented but also quite determined, Billy assessed, and what harm could it do? He had to admit to liking her enthusiasm and energy too. Who knows, maybe it would even rub off on him.

"Okay. Let me just turn the sign for a bit. We don't want anyone coming in when we're halfway through. It isn't normally busy at this time anyway."

He moved from behind the counter, shuffled over to the door, flipped the hanging "Open" sign and slowly started to move displays of plastic animals away from the window.

"Let me get that one with you. We don't want them breaking up and all the contents spilling out. Actually, that's given me an idea. Don't you have a set of farm buildings somewhere?"

They spent the next two hours constructing a farmyard in one window and zoo in the other as centre pieces, with appropriately themed animal games and puzzles around and soft toys above. Billy patiently passed the items to Ellie while she knelt or stood, almost doubled over, on the ledges in the windows. She even found a balloon animal making set, similar to one she and Simon had played with years back, and twisted some rather good models, with stuck-on eyes, noses and mouths cut out of felt, which she suspended from string even higher in the window. After checking with Billy, she also emptied a box of delible felt-tip pens and drew pictures around the bottom and side edges of the glass. She carefully placed the open box and all pens, apparently scattered randomly but actually in a beautiful criss-cross pattern, in the front right-hand corner of the right window. They worked silently, apart from the odd question, suggestion or small cry of inspiration or appreciation as ideas unfolded in front of their eyes. The shop bell rang approvingly, as Billy repeatedly passed through it to point, nod, mouth silent words, gesture approval or otherwise and generally orchestrate the transformation, while Ellie stepped about behind the glass, increasingly more carefully and on higher tiptoes.

After his final re-entry into the shop, Billy disappeared into the back again and returned, grinning, with a string of small solar lights, usually only produced just before Christmas.

"Well, it's not that far off, is it, and it's dark enough now of an evening that they'll catch people's eyes as they pass by."

Their glow was negligible at first but by the time Ellie climbed back down into the shop, back, neck and arms aching and fingers sore from manipulating and tying rubber, they were coming alive, blinking against the grey morning.

Ellie and Billy were blinking too, trying to absorb their achievement. They were both flushed and slightly breathless. Ellie's baseball cap was gummed to her hair and head, from the effort of inspiration, careful, tense movement and, let's face it, excitement. Billy himself hadn't enjoyed himself as much since the newest model railway had arrived at the shop. Of course, the model railway, why hadn't he thought of that! Maybe they could get it out and set it up in the shop; that would get the youngsters interested, maybe even the parents too. These days, a lot of older people were getting into model trains as a hobby too.

"I'd best be going," said Ellie. "I need to get to the cycle shop."

Billy tried to hide his disappointment. "Can't I even get you a cuppa? It's the least I can do after all your hard work."

"Thank you. It's tempting, but I said I'd pick something up this morning. I don't want Greg to think I'm not coming. If you don't mind, I'd like to come back some time though, to see whether the change makes any difference?"

"Of course. I'd like that. But I don't even know your name? I'm Billy, Billy Anderson." He held out his hand.

"Hi, Billy Anderson. I'm Ellie Coley. Nice to meet you. Look forward to seeing you again."

They shook hands and smiled at each other.

# 3

"What in heaven's name…?"

In the gift shop opposite Billy Anderson's toy shop, an open-mouthed Maureen Enderby was steaming up the window glass, her suntanned, lined face closely pressed against it. Over the road she could see, immediately below the colourful name sign, legging-bound limbs, crouched, then slowly and carefully extending, one after the other, across the window, gingerly touching down and contracting again into a squat; while arms, previously spread aloft in balance, came slowly and gracefully down to rest on the floor, fingers spread, for all the world like a goddess of the surrounding toys, performing a slow-motion, ritual dance to bring them alive. Only then could Maureen see the baseball cap on top.

Someone walked past her shop and looked at Maureen staring through the window. She hastily made a motion as though to clean the glass, inspected the spot closely again and turned away to continue dusting.

*I'll need to keep an eye on that*, she thought to herself.

Maureen rigorously and jealously guarded the reputation not only of herself, her husband Frank, her own small, quaint and moderately successful gift shop but the reputation of the high street, which meant, of course, that she had the right to know the business of all shopkeepers there. This heartfelt duty was all the more intensified by Maureen being one of the very few property owners, rather than leaseholders, on the street, having inherited a DIY shop from her father. It was also intricately entwined with a fierce determination to continue her annual two-week holidays in Crete, funded by gift shop profits.

This is what had led to the recent feud with Chrissy, the florist, who had had the temerity to add locally made costume jewellery and other crafts to her stock, even going so far (so far!) as to display them in the window. Maureen had marched straight in, flabbergasted, on passing one morning to reach her own premises, and demanded to know what Chrissy was up to and was she trying to undermine her own, Maureen's, hard-won and long-standing family business?

To Maureen's obvious and intense irritation and afront, Chrissy had only been slightly defensive: she was stocking only a very few, choice items, mainly to provide an outlet for a friend. She wasn't aware that she needed to obtain anyone's permission to do so. Maureen flounced out of the florist's after retorting words to the effect that Chrissy had better make sure it stayed that way as she, Maureen, had influence on the council. On reflection, and after she'd managed to calm down, she felt a little bit bad about that, given the poor girl's difficult circumstances.

Maureen dusted the phone. Her older customers had landlines, often instead of mobile phones, and were, on the whole, suspicious of technology, so she had retained both the phone itself and the number from her father. Maureen particularly appreciated the solidity of the old phone – no one's going to break or lose that one, unlike the kids of today with their flimsy little toys, sticking out of back pockets (this, no doubt, with one of her five grandchildren in mind). She even occasionally still got calls asking about paint and tools and whether she delivered free locally. She enjoyed these chats with descendants of her father's customers, who admitted, apologetically, to coming across the entry in a dilapidated address book, but they remembered well how highly Dad/Grandad had spoken of Joe. In particular, she could stress that the shop remained in the family because it was owned by the family and offer a 20% discount on their first visit to the gift shop. That usually meant they did actually come in, mostly in a fit of curiosity and nostalgia – a very conducive frame of mind for purchasing photo frames for deceased loved ones or books about the history of the town, with fuzzy, black-and-white photos of shops in various guises, including hers, of course – she knew the page numbers by heart.

Maureen hesitated. She had a strict policy of using the phone for business purposes only – a customer could be trying to get in touch, after all. "But this *is* business," she murmured to herself, picking up the receiver and dialling a local number.

"Bridget, it's Maureen. Do you know if there's anything going on at the toy shop over the road? I've seen some strange activity this morning. Like a refit, or bizarre stock take. A complete change of window display and what looks like a teenage girl doing it with Billy's help. I didn't think he had a granddaughter, did you?"

"I'm sure he doesn't. There's only Susan and that wayward son, Harry, isn't it, who went off to sea and the Middle East and God knows where else? Unless Andy's got a girlfriend and she's helping out? Can't really believe it though, he's such a gawky, spotty so and so. Mind you, there's no accounting for taste, is there? Leave it with me. I've a friend who knows the sister of someone who works at the council. I'm just having coffee with Angie and then I'll get onto it."

Maureen carefully replaced the receiver and felt safe to walk to the front of the shop again to take another look. The road was quite busy now with passing traffic and pedestrians and she had to strain to see. She didn't have as good a view of the left window front opposite as she did of the right because the gift shop was on a slight bend in the road, but she could swear that much the same activity was now happening there. She watched while Billy exited the shop a few times to gesticulate to the person inside the window. It was like a silent pantomime.

Frustratingly, some customers entered the shop. Maureen put her best face on, greeted them warmly, asked after their morning, began her usual spiel about the shop heritage and asked whether they were local or just visiting. "As I know most of the locals by sight, of course, you see." Having established they were tourists, and reasonably well-dressed ones at that, looking for presents, Maureen directed them to the souvenir prints (too expensive, she deduced), candles (pushing it a bit), tea towels (too utilitarian), mugs (maybe a good compromise) and engraved glasses. "These are very popular. You should have some yourselves as well. There's nothing like reminiscing about where you've been on holiday when you're having a drink of an evening."

Later, Maureen sat down, exhausted but satisfied with her sales, a cup of tea resting on her ample midriff. Despite the feeling of job well done, she felt her knees aching and feet throbbing. *I need to get out that foot massager Cecily bought me for Christmas*, she thought as she heaved herself up to answer the phone's ancient, insistent ringing.

"Maureen, it's me, Bridget. I've found out all about it. There's a competition, sponsored by the council, for the best shopfront at Christmas! Them at the toy shop must be experimenting or practicing or something."

"What, a competition? So, there's money, or something, for the winner?"

"Yes! £5,000!"

Maureen couldn't help a gasp, visualising Crete in all its glories, at several times of the year.

"Bridget, you've got to help me. We have to enter and win!"

# 4

Chrissy Dickson unlocked, opened and wheeled herself into her florist shop, not without difficulty, in a reflective mood that morning.

She'd had the shop for just over a year now, and she had always promised herself that she would make the decision, a year on from starting, whether to carry on or throw in the towel, depending on the success, or otherwise, of her venture. The problem was that the shop had been neither a roaring success nor a dismal failure. Profits were there, but certainly not substantial, and was it really worth all the hassle and stress if she wasn't making herself, well, even ever so slightly wealthy, to compensate for it?

Maybe she owed it to her dad, who'd loaned her money to help pay for the first year of the lease, to hang on a bit longer. And, to be fair, she'd been well received by the townspeople who were, almost without exception, kind and considerate.

Even the delivery men, who offloaded the flowers for her shop, had been incredibly receptive to her, rather stammering, request early on to stand the crates where she pointed them so she could easily see inside. They'd even insisted on extracting her flowers from the Cellophane inside the crates and laying them on the counter so she could easily sort and put them into her buckets. She'd tried to tip the driver, the older of the men, motioning that he should share the money with his colleague but, with a disturbingly old-fashioned but charming doffing of his cap, he'd smiled and politely refused. He mumbled something about having a daughter of about her age and liking to think that people would help her, as she started out in the world, in the same sort of way, and gratis.

*What a shame everyone can't be that nice,* Chrissy mused as she busied herself with the usual routine of cancelling the alarm, turning on the till, pulling on her apron, dropping her hand into the buckets to check water levels and perusing the order book for any special bouquets, wreaths or centrepieces required for the day. Her last job every day was to check the book, but she always looked again the following morning, as though one of the large yuccas might have come alive in the night and mischievously made its own addendum with spiky fingers. Just one centrepiece required this week, and she'd be better leaving it for the morning it was required: purple/red protea, orange safari sunset, red hypericum berry, white wax flower, gold chrysanthemum and something else lighter to set off the purples and reds. Yellow gerbera, perhaps? She made a note in the book to add some to the order later. At least it wasn't a delivery day today; that made things a lot easier.

Chrissy scrutinised the array of buckets on the floor at the side, went over and extracted a couple of flowers from each and put them in an empty one, adding green foliage from another and water from a can by the sink. She then dragged the bucket of mixed blooms to the side of the counter, so she wouldn't accidentally sell them in the day. After which, she could sit for a minute at the counter and fill her lungs with that intoxicating, combined scent of numerous fresh autumn flowers, damp earth, grasses, wood and paper, and her own potpourri. *Her* smell.

Yes, the episode with Maureen Enderby had been rather disturbing. Chrissy hadn't said anything to her dad, in case it made him want to take the matter into his own hands, but it rankled all the more for being unshared. She'd offered to Debbie to put the necklaces and earrings in her shop window, more as an experiment than anything else as Debbie was seriously doubtful that they were any good. But a few had been snatched up, accompanied by very complimentary comments from customers on the beauty and style of the pieces. These, of course, she'd shared with Debbie, and when Debbie had wanted to give her a cut of the proceeds, Chrissy had refused, saying they had brought people into the shop, one of whom had added potpourri to her order, to complete the birthday gift. Debbie was pleased but only half convinced that Chrissy wasn't telling fibs.

*If we less able-bodied people can't help each other, how can we expect anyone else to?* she asked herself, as she at last switched on the kettle and dropped a teabag into the portable cup she could attach to her chair. *And I certainly can't tell Debbie about Maureen as she'd feel responsible and not give me any more stuff. And why should we give in to an interfering old bat like her?*

At which point, a customer came in for a small "thank you for looking after my cat" bouquet. Chrissy wheeled circles around the flowers, like a bumble bee, sheet of paper on her lap ready to receive the blooms and greenery, surveying and suggesting vibrant lilies and roses, offset by deep coloured foliage. She took the assembled offering to her low, wooden desk, reverentially lifted the sheet, full of its fragrant burden, from her lap onto its surface and began the process she loved best of all.

While constructing a bouquet, Chrissy was always silent: forehead furrowed with concentration and head tilting to one side then the other, judging the effects as much as to get a slightly better view, fingers working quickly and noiselessly to trim and knit the stalks together, pull off unnecessary or unwanted material, arrange the colours to best advantage and, finally, bind, wrap and seal the creation. She smiled and patted it gently, pulled out the drawer under the desk, found the compartment she was looking for and fished out a small, oblong card.

Chrissy smiled up, a little smugly, at the customer and said, "It's a cat card. You can tell your friend the flowers are from your cat."

The woman laughed. "Thank you, I hadn't thought of that. She will be chuffed. Thank you, it's a beautiful bouquet."

She paid and left. Chrissy carefully pulled together the corners of the sheet on her desk, scrunched them closed and dropped the resulting pyramid into her lap, wheeled round to two recycling bins against the wall, emptied the discarded, mainly green, contents into one and dropped the screwed-up paper into the other. With a deep feeling of satisfaction that always followed the making of a good-sized bouquet, Chrissy returned to making her cup of tea.

Much later, and with another cup of tea in hand, Chrissy glided to the front of the shop and looked through the slightly befogged window. It was grey, a little damp but rain-free outside. A pale, nebulous sun was bravely trying to battle through the clouds. Chrissy's attention was suddenly caught by a small, slight, silver-haired woman in leggings, cycle jacket and baseball cap in hand, and a bulky-looking rucksack slung over her shoulder, cycle helmet bouncing underneath, marching past the shop.

"Goodness, it's a bit chilly not to have your jacket on, Granny," Chrissy murmured, "and I wonder why you're in such a hurry."

She took a slow sip of tea, somewhat absent-mindedly.

*More lovely, really appreciative customers today. At least the odds are going the right way*, she thought to herself. And then out loud, "Maybe I'll give us another six months, eh, shop?"

# 5

"Hi, Greg, sorry I'm late."

Ellie bounced into the cycle shop, nearly crashing into a Madone propped up near the door for repair. Greg flew out from the back of the shop to rescue it.

"My fault, sorry, Ellie, for leaving it there," Greg replied as he saw her petrified face. "I haven't had time to move it to the back. I really need more space. Do you want a cuppa, and how's the Trek?"

*Typical of Greg,* she thought, *very kind to try and distract me. So different from Simon, and yet not much younger.*

Greg looked more like a biker than a cyclist, she often thought, with his neatly trimmed beard and dark hair pulled back into a short ponytail. He looked as she'd always imagined one of the three, or four, Musketeers would look, and she'd immediately liked him for it.

He'd shared some of his story with her: not really remembering his real parents at all, the years in care, dedicated but eventually frustrated and angry foster parents, various school expulsions, drugs and then, finally, on one of the days when he actually did drag himself into school, a gold-medal-winning cyclist giving a talk.

The celebrity cyclist talked about his life story, not so vastly different from Greg's own, and about the relatively harmless addiction of road and off-road cycling. The pictures that flashed up on the screen said it all. Endless space, filled by sky, mountains, trees, fields, grazing animals, rivers and the long, long road ahead. Greg had gone home, mesmerised, and startled his foster parents by asking if they would loan him the money to buy a second-hand bike he'd seen on eBay. He would pay them back in monthly instalments or do any jobs about the house to pay in kind. Bemused, but quietly ecstatic, they agreed to lend the money.

The road hadn't been entirely straight, with plenty of dead ends, roundabouts, U-turns and roadworks on the way. From time to time, he'd slipped back into drugs, mainly following jeering taunts from his "mates", but he never let up on paying his foster parents back.

He took up a paper round, comfortable in the knowledge that none of his mates would be up early enough to see him and, after all, it was good use of the bike. He actually came to love those early mornings, pushing along through the cold, newborn day, pausing to deliver, throwing himself up onto the bike again, electrifying himself through repeated stopping and starting, impulsion and rhythm.

He worked at the local DIY store at weekends as well, again, somewhere his mates would never set foot. He pushed heavy trolleys, from lorry in the bay to warehouse inside, and stacked shelves at night. They were impressed by his hard work and dedication and asked if he'd like to be promoted to a job at front. Painfully aware of the pay increase he was rejecting, he bit his lip and declined but asked for more shifts to make up the difference. They accepted and later even offered him a small increase in his hourly rate.

Within a year, Greg had paid for the bike. He was ecstatic. Then disaster occurred. On rounding the corner from the warehouse building into the loading bay one lunchtime, Greg met Gizza, sitting on one of the unloaded boxes, smoking a joint.

"Hi, Greg, how you doing?"

Greg gestured towards the CCTV camera sign at the side of the bay door. "You can't do that here, Gizza, you'll be seen. Have a care, mate."

Gizza eyed him up and then the sign.

"Nah, those things are never working. Anyway, I know they're not, cos my dad works here. That's how I found out about you, the model employee."

Mimicking his father's voice, he continued, "In the manager's office, he was. Offered a better deal but declined. Didn't want to work in the shop. Such a shame, he's a really good lad. You could take a leaf out of his book, Gary."

Gizza smirked and coughed at the same time on his joint, his long legs splayed against the side of the box, his upper body rocking left and right in amusement. "Anyways, I thought I'd come and see the model employee for myself."

Gizza jumped down, slightly unsteadily and, righting himself, walked as purposefully as he could up to Greg until they were nose to nose with each other. The acrid smell of marijuana exuded from his clothes and breath.

"What you doing here, you crackhead? You're no better than me. You'll see what I can do to my dad's model employee."

The flash of light on blade appeared before Greg was even aware of the source. It was held high against the midday sun. Greg thought, *this is it, I've had it*, but Gizza continued to hold it aloft and, laughing and prancing around his prey, like a demonic disciple, he baited his victim, thrusting here and there, left to right playfully, while Greg nimbly dodged around machinery, pallets and boxes.

Until Gizza spied Greg's shiny bike, carefully attached with its padlock to the fence at the side of the bay. Greg saw his eyes slant in that direction and moved protectively towards it, holding both arms up in submission. "No, mate, please leave it alone, it's all I've got." Greg had never begged before, but now he really felt like dropping to his knees, in total submission, to try to avert what he knew was about to happen.

No good. Gizza pushed past him, swaying and threatening him with the knife again, crouched and gleefully applied the knife to both front and back tyres, ripping the rubber asunder like a drunken mortician and singing all the time under his breath the lyrics of Queen's *Bicycle Race*.

White-hot rage gripped Greg so that, for a few seconds,

he could neither move nor breathe. Gizza stood up and proudly surveyed his handiwork. He turned to Greg to gloat some more, but then his expression changed, as in a slow-motion film, from manic amusement to stupefaction, then slow and dim comprehension, followed by bald fear. His eyes filled his face, pupils dilated, and tiny beads of sweat popped out of the skin on his forehead.

For a few split seconds totally oblivious to the knife, still glittering in the sun, Greg lunged. He caught Gizza off guard and, in any case, his opponent was too stoned to move quickly. His hands were round the other boy's neck, squeezing as tightly as he could until Gizza's eyes looked as though they would explode. Greg heard the knife hit the concrete but ignored it and carried on, now shaking Gizza back and forth while holding him as though this would speed up the process of eking every last breath out of him.

He never knew what would have happened next if one of the workers hadn't come running out of the warehouse, yelling at him to let go and trying, with difficulty, to separate them. Another followed him, without whom the outcome could have been very different as the first man was failing in his struggle to pull Greg away.

Gizza dropped like a stone, his knees folding underneath him, and was only saved from cracking his skull on the ground by the man who held him up, having at last, with his co-worker's help, extracted Greg's hands from around his neck. He laid Gizza down as gently as he could, staggering and panting himself, pulled out his mobile phone, jabbed a number and stammered hoarsely to demand an ambulance. The second man held Greg as tightly as he could, not convinced he wouldn't have another go.

Unfortunately, Gizza was right, the CCTV wasn't working. In court, Gizza, prominent in his neck brace, admitted he'd slashed Greg's tyres because Greg had been bullying him all the while and boasting about his new bike. He alleged he'd done it before Greg came out of the building, meaning to be gone before anyone saw so he'd also have the satisfaction of Greg never knowing who'd vandalised his precious bike. Greg had come out, found him doing it and attacked him from behind. Yes, he'd taken drugs, but that was to give him the courage to do the job – he was by nature (and many attested to this) quite a timid lad.

Despite testaments – from foster parents, other warehouse staff and teachers – to Greg's good character, hard work, commitment and gentle nature, Gizza's rescuers had to admit that they really thought Greg might have killed him if they hadn't arrived on the scene.

Greg went to a juvenile detention centre for four years. During sentencing the judge confessed he was being lenient due to this being Greg's first offence, unlike his *victim* (placing extra emphasis on the word, as though he wasn't entirely convinced, and throwing an ironic look at Gizza), the many good character statements provided and his behaviour on the day in question being totally out of keeping with his general demeanour up to that point. Despite having two dependable and corroborating eye-witness accounts of the attack, which was indeed shocking in itself, the absence of CCTV footage (throwing a hard stare at the warehouse manager who'd attended the trial to support his two worker witnesses) to show what had led up to it was, well, extremely disappointing, dissatisfying and disturbing. He could not bring himself to pass down a sentence that would send Greg to an adult prison as a very young man; that never helped anyone, least of all society and the prisoner himself.

Despite previous run-ins with the police over drugs, Gizza got only ten days' community service for possession and use. Greg would play the scene over in his head time after time, not just to the psychologist, over those four years. Would he have? He honestly didn't know and, worse still, he didn't know whether he cared. His foster parents were kind, visiting him two or three times a week, despite the distance, and assuring him he could come back to them.

One of the best things about prison was the bike in the gym. Greg used it every day and built up his fitness in readiness for returning to the real thing. He never did drugs again, though they were available if he'd wanted them. The smaller class sizes and more intense teaching also suited him, and he came out with decent qualifications, including in physical education and business management.

A careers advisor helped Greg draft a letter and business proposal to apply for a loan from his bank to set up business as a bicycle sale and repair shop. His foster parents had already committed to investing in the business with some of their savings: "With interest rates being so low, the return should be higher than keeping it in the bank, and if we make more than expected, we'll happily plough it back into the business. It's just up to you,

Greg, to make a good go of it."

His mum and dad also helped convince the bank manager that, despite his criminal record, Greg would be a model customer and, in any case, they were there to support and guarantee repayment. He'd never really looked back.

There'd been setbacks, of course, but his foster parents and bank manager remained largely supportive. Cycling became a popular sport as environmental issues and fuel costs pricked people's consciousness and pockets; electric bikes flourished and government helped fund purchases; paths began to appear everywhere, the local council committing to create more. The time it took for Greg's business to establish itself meant that more and more customers weren't aware of his past and took him at face value, for the knowledgeable, able and conscientious young shop holder he was.

Eventually, business was doing so well that Greg left his foster parents' house for a small rented furnished flat not far from the high street. It was a wrench for them all. After both helped him clean the flat and move in, there was an awkward farewell, even though they would only be a fifteen-minute ride away and he'd promised to go to dinner every Monday when the shop was shut. Even Dad had tears in his eyes, strongly asserting they were of pride as much as anything, and gave him a rather stiff bear hug. Mum was openly weeping, and it was as much as Greg could do to hold himself together.

There was a moment of panic, too, when they finally closed the door behind them. What had he done and how in hell was he going to cope on his own? But he'd surprised himself with how easy it was. Okay, despite his protestations, Mum came weekly to "give the flat a quick going over" while he was at the shop, and from time to time brought a plant, which she promised to water as he would likely forget. If she pried into his things while she was there, he didn't care, though he did make sure to dispose very carefully of any used condoms after one of his few female visitors stayed the night. She did ask about girlfriends one day, possibly after detecting residual scent in the flat but, after he evaded the question, she tactfully didn't ask again. He didn't really care for any of them; it was just downtime from the pressures, and stresses at accounts time, of the shop.

The only other person who'd been to the flat was Ellie. He'd felt shy about inviting her, but it was when he'd accidentally let slip about his pending twenty-first birthday. She'd suggested a drink at the pub, but Greg avoided locations where old "mates" might hang out, so he replied by asking if she'd like to see the flat. He knew immediately she was both surprised and flattered as she coloured up and stammered her delight and acceptance.

She'd brought a bottle of wine, some beers and snacks and a bottle opener in the shape of a bike as a birthday gift, apologising that it was only small as she needed to fit it into her rucksack. His card was also a pop-up with cyclist, saying "Happy twenty-first, Greg. Just keep pedalling! Love from Ellie". She'd agonised over that but decided that "best wishes" or "regards" were just too formal; she'd rather commit the sin of overfamiliarity than boringness.

After a couple of beers, he opened up about his past; he hadn't intended to but, as it was his birthday celebration, Ellie naturally asked a few questions about previous occasions. Unlike with Mum, he didn't feel the need to hold back with Ellie, though he couldn't quite put his finger on why. Maybe it was because she hadn't been there, and he hadn't hurt her.

She was a really good listener, not reacting at all, apart from leaning further forwards and briefly snatching air into her mouth when he got to the Gizza part. She didn't even ask whether he'd intended to commit murder, and he didn't offer anything, just described what had happened and how he'd been punished. Somehow, he managed to explain to her, which he never properly had to Mum or Dad, why he didn't feel angry about the punishment, only with Gizza, because it was deserved and it had got him away from the gang and the drugs. What might have happened if not?

When she left, she took his hand at the door, stretched up on tiptoes and kissed him, very lightly, on the cheek, saying "happy birthday" again. She gave his hand a squeeze before letting go as well. Greg hadn't even been surprised and bent his head slightly to receive the kiss; it just felt like the natural thing for them both to do.

She'd invited herself, and he'd invited her, a few times after that; it was as though neither of them wanted that to be the only shared experience there. She'd invited him to hers too, but he'd always declined, saying he'd rather her at his, given he had so few visitors there. And he was allergic to cats (he didn't even know whether this was true, having never been that close to one).

Now, here she was, inadvertently wrecking his shop

for him. He smiled to himself, picked up the Madone easily by handlebar and down tube, headed towards the back of the shop and threw over his shoulder, "I'll put the kettle on and get your lights. I've got biscuits too. We can settle down and put our thinking caps on about this local council shop window display competition. I want to enter it as it'll be good for business and, if I win, I can put the money towards expanding the shop. I need your help with ideas."

# 6

Berk Arsian was third generation Turk. He affected an accent and flamboyant gestures to provide much expected, and appreciated, authenticity to his clients, but he was British, born and bred, and proud of it.

Berk's great-grandfather had fled with his young family when Kemal assumed power, having spoken out in favour of Sultan Mehmed. He'd been shopped by another barber, newly arrived in town and anxious to establish business.

The family had never returned and, over generations, became radically Anglophile, adopting a flexible and pragmatic approach to religious celebrations, so that, while shunning alcohol and honouring both Eids, they shared and sent small presents at Christmas, largely because other people gave to them. In time Berk's wife, Defne, also decided they would call their first daughter Lola. The boys, Yusuf and Kaan, had had his naming, after his father and grandfather, and now it was her turn. Berk, always wanting an easy life, particularly with Def, agreed.

Lola was his precious *kizim*, his *prenses*, his *canim*, his *aşkım*, his *tatlim*. He loved his sons too, of course, but since Lola was born, Berk was captivated, in a way never before, even with Def. When those tiny fingers tightened round his seemingly huge proffered forefinger with an unexpected strength, and the dark, oval eyes stared inquisitively and defiantly up at him, it was as though an iron fist clenched his heart and twisted it inside out.

Strict with the boys, he was overindulgent with her, to Def's chagrin and not insubstantial attacks of jealousy. As these resulted in irritability, the bond between father and daughter strengthened. It was Berk who taxied her round to parties, dancing classes and swimming lessons and attended every school event.

He and Def had agreed they wanted her to go to a single-sex school, so this meant the local Catholic primary, somewhere in days gone past she would never have been admitted, but there was a liberal headmistress and declining Catholic population in the town.

Lola loved it there because she was viewed as different, verging on the exotic, and became queen of a small group of girls who considered themselves cosmopolitan intellectuals. They loved coming to her house for its colourful and comfortable decor, delicious home cooking, particularly sweets, and stories from Berk about his great-grandfather's time in Turkey, spread and spiced up in much the same way as the food. Inevitably, the girls' parents were asked in at collection time and some became customers.

Def relished the occasions too, the girls hanging onto

her every word about Turkish food, cooking methods and clothes; she went as far as reweighting her wardrobe of one *şalvar* versus the balance of Western dress, initiating squeals of delight and a barrage of questions on opening the front door to her young, female guests. Berk was rigidly strict about his boys' behaviour around the girls, feeling as protective of them as he would have been of Lola in the same situation. In fact, rarely did Lola go to any of her friends' houses as they all wanted to come to her, complaining of boring parents, dinners and interrogations.

Lola did well at school and agreed to progress to the, rather distant, single-sex Catholic high school. She was astute enough to know that she'd get a better and more enjoyable education there without the distraction and cattiness induced by boys. The sixth form was mixed though; a forward-thinking and pragmatic move some years before by the then Reverend Mother Headmistress and Master of the boys' senior school.

Having flown high through her exams, Lola settled on a university and degree in medicine. She was now in her fifth year of six. Berk wasn't physically capable of concealing his pride when customers asked after her, nor his worry about her dealings with the opposite sex. She'd dated a few fellow students but no more, according to her. She was too busy with mates, some old schoolfriends; too engrossed in her work; they were too immature, too obsessed with football, too boringly political, too interested in only talking about themselves. Berk and Def had no choice but to believe her.

The boys had long left home, following decidedly

undramatic school and college careers. They were more practical, like their father. Yusuf was a joiner, married to a boisterous Liverpudlian who, being an orphaned, only child, had embraced his family as her own and made them love her for it. Kaan was a successful painter/decorator with a trainee teacher girlfriend he'd been seeing for about six months: by far the longest relationship he'd had so far, so Berk and Def were cautiously optimistic but at the same time trepidatious as he'd only brought her home a few times. Berk often regretted that neither boy had shown any interest in carrying on the family trade; however, there was time yet, he supposed.

In the children's, and particularly Lola's, absence, Berk had thrown himself back into work. The shop was well established and profitable, thanks to his father finally buying the premises; Berk had recruited and trained two new members of staff and paid off the mortgage on the house.

He adored both the business and his customers, never losing the excitement of starting a new day and wondering what it might bring, as he allowed walk-in appointments as well. He particularly loved hot towel shaving and beard trimming as they provoked the quickest and most enthusiastic responses from new customers in particular, and that meant they almost always came back and often bought gift vouchers for fussy friends and relations: "Oh, man, that felt so good, thanks a lot, Berk."

This morning, Berk opened the shop somewhat absent-mindedly, leaflet in hand and with a perplexed expression on his face. How on earth could he create a picturesque, eye-catching and relevant window display in a barber's shop? The mind boggled: grooming implements arrayed, like instruments of torture; disembodied heads with wigs, trimmed to various lengths and styles; a garish and tacky depiction of Turkish life, complete with confectionery? He was at a loss.

Luckily, it was a busy day with long-established customers, so, to a certain extent, he could afford to go onto autopilot. Fred, for a trim, with his disapproving tales of unruly grandchildren and lazy parenting; Terry, for a shave and trim, with stories of how he was going to make it big in the music world one day; Steve, with a hair and beard trim, who was debating whether to start dyeing his hair after finding silver streaks at the age of twenty-eight; young Johnny, for a trim, who was brought in by his dad and wanted to be an astronaut, when it was a fireman last time; Gordon, as fastidious as ever, for his usual makeover of shave, trim and facial hair removal, accompanied by painful recounts of long-lost love affairs with other male extras he'd met on location (Berk often wondered whether he should charge a psychiatrist's fee); then Cyril, a lovable old man, living on his own, who came in every week and actually wanted a proper conversation, so Berk happily obliged.

They'd talk about anything: politics, the state of the roads or refuse collection in town, economics, Berk's family (Cyril had none) and business and Cyril's wife, deceased fifteen years ago. Even now Cyril's eyes would become filmy while he related old anecdotes of them ballroom dancing (that's how they'd met), cruising round the world (that's why no children: the brochures just kept dropping through the door, and Edith had enough of them at the school where she worked) or winning at bingo or on the horses and what they did with the proceeds.

"Mind you," Cyril's eyes lit up at the consoling thought, "she'd have loved that window display in the toy shop along the road: you know, the one with the animals centre stage. She'd have said, 'The kids at school will love that.' Berk was confused but too polite, or embarrassed, to express it.

His next appointment had been cancelled. Berk hadn't had a break all day and the weather wasn't bad, so he pulled on his coat, offering to get anything required by anybody, customers included, from the deli, and left the shop. Fresh air, after the heat, steam and product smells, as much as he loved them, was invigorating, and Berk walked briskly along the street, greeting people as he went. The toy shop was no more than two hundred metres away.

Cyril had been right: the scenes were captivating. Berk could put on his child's eyes and see them in all their glory, magnified by the dull, grey day behind him, as he bent to look more closely. He studied both windows slowly and then stopped, his attention snatched by an animal in the zoo, a camel. His mind flew back, over years, to all those school shows, concerts and events in which Lola had not only participated but played a major role. She was such a quietly confident, self-possessed child and young woman, who threw herself whole-heartedly into everything she did, that the staff knew she would commit, work hard, learn her lines and, of course, look amazing in any role she took on. There had been so many that it seemed the pictures would never cease transmuting themselves in Berk's head, but suddenly his memory stopped, like an old-fashioned newsreel, at a particular one.

Lola had been allocated the role of wise woman in a Christmas show at senior school, quite a milestone and emotional event for Berk and Defne in particular, as it was her last. She was the only female of the three wise people, which in itself made her stand out from them and the rest of the cast. She'd been chosen for her acting and speaking talent, of course, and given a long speech (the longest of the show) about where they had come from, where they were going and why, but also because of her dark hair and eyes, clear, olive skin, exotic appearance and slow, elegant, regal movement while she spoke, captivating the audience with her story, resplendent in brightly coloured robes and shining crown, frankincense in a gold goblet in hand. Even the two-person camel, muffling grunts and giggles behind, didn't distract her or detract from the performance. She was a sensation: the comments from teachers and other parents after the show still echoed in Berk's head.

Berk's strained, intense look slowly dissolved into a smile. He knew exactly what he was going to do.

# 7

Fran and Beth, who ran the bookshop together, had been emotional, then romantic, partners for years before they became business ones. They often reminisced to their younger gay friends that they were so old they were probably at least partly responsible for inventing gay female relationships in the UK.

It was certainly true they'd got together not only long before it became "fashionable" (as Fran laughingly called it) to be gay but also when it was considered distinctly antisocial, if not a downright public danger. They had been teachers and therefore all the more discreet to start with, not even letting on that they lived together. Beth gave her aunt's address as her own, for the school records. The aunt obliged because she appreciated the frequent visits to collect school-related post, when Beth was astute and grateful enough to drink tea and gossip with her. She was actually also deeply fond of her, knowing her to be a woman who noticed everything but didn't talk indiscreetly about people she cared for.

Fran and Beth had worked at different, though reasonably close, schools. They'd met at an educational conference in Edinburgh, in the hotel bar after a long and intensive day of talks, seminars, role play and heated discussions about the merits, or otherwise, of a constructivist versus behaviourist approach. Fran walked up to Beth's table, where she was nursing a gin and tonic, and asked if she could join her with her white wine and soda and proffered nibbles. She'd clocked Beth in the corner while buying her own drink and quickly added two packets of crisps to her order. Of course, Beth said yes, curious about the rather flamboyantly dressed woman she'd noticed in the auditorium.

Fran had, very firmly and eloquently, Beth admiringly thought, rebutted some of the expert opinions of the speaker, citing her own experiences and outcomes. Beth agreed with much of what she said but was too shy to support her other than under her breath. She told Fran this now, apologetically, who laughed and made reference to the opinionated young man who was scarcely out of nursery.

Beth asked her to elaborate on the experiences she'd mentioned, and Fran obliged, concisely but with feeling. She talked about children she'd helped through the most difficult of circumstances at home and school, working with them until she found a method that made them connect and engage and which was different in almost all cases. Theories were all well and good, but you couldn't, and shouldn't, compartmentalise children. Beth listened intently, anxious to learn. She was about ten years younger than Fran and grateful for the attention and information.

They had dinner together in an Italian restaurant near the hotel and exchanged addresses and phone numbers. To their mutual surprise, they lived and worked not far away from each other. They got into the habit of meeting at a local restaurant once a month, and later going to the cinema or theatre, when there was something on that was inviting because it was good or ridiculous. If the latter, they occasionally got threatened with expulsion from the cinema or theatre.

Then one Christmas, Fran let slip that she would be spending it alone as she was parentless, without siblings and all her friends had other plans. Usually, she went to a neighbour, but the neighbour was going to be away, visiting her daughter and new grandchild. Beth was horrified. She always went to her aunt, who didn't like to travel, particularly in the winter, and Beth's parents had either her sister or brother, with their children, at theirs. Beth visited them on Boxing Day instead, when they exchanged presents. She was sure her aunt would be happy to have Fran too, particularly as they both mucked in with the cooking – it wasn't as though it would be more work for her, in fact less, with three pairs of hands instead of two. Beth's aunt agreed. She'd heard all about Fran and was glad Beth had her as a friend. She was also curious to meet her, given Beth had spoken so much about her.

Christmas day was a huge success. Fran got on with Beth's aunt like a house on fire, teasing and joking with her, and doing instantly recognisable impressions of the various staff members at her school, some of whom the aunt knew. They all ate and drank too much and then

Beth's aunt asked if they'd like to stay over, the weather being as awful as it was; Beth usually did anyway. Fran admitted she didn't relish the thought of the walk home, but she had nothing with her. Beth said she could remedy that, no problem, as she always left stuff at her aunt's.

Her aunt, more than slightly tipsy, went to bed at 10.00. Beth and Fran continued to sit downstairs on the sofa together, drinking coffee and watching Christmas day evening repeats on TV, not wanting to move. Emboldened by the alcohol and grateful to Fran for giving her aunt the best day she'd had in years, Beth put her own hand down on Fran's, lying on the sofa between them. She didn't say thank you, she didn't need to; Fran knew exactly what she meant. She responded by curling her own hand round Beth's and holding it tight. Not looking at her, light flickering on her face from the TV in the nearly dark room, Fran then lifted Beth's hand to her face and kissed it, slowly and longingly. Beth immediately knew what she meant: "I did it for you because I love you and I want you."

They kissed on the first-floor landing, giggling outside Beth's aunt's room at the sound of deep and sonorous snoring. It was a kiss of blissful recognition and acceptance, excitement for the future but resignation for the night ahead. Beth pointed Fran in the direction of her room and the bathroom and disappeared into her own room, turning at the door to blow another kiss with her hand. "Soon.", she mouthed.

And it had been, at Fran's flat, bought with her parents' legacy but still leaving substantial savings. To give themselves cover, Fran invited a few friends and neighbours for a drinks and quiz evening. Beth feigned a migraine towards the end of the evening and the guests politely departed, hoping she would feel better soon: "I'm sure I will, thank you." Fran had said she'd better stay over as she was in no fit state to go anywhere.

Beth made a miraculous recovery as soon as everyone was safely away and led Fran upstairs, smiling wickedly.

They'd been together ever since, Beth eventually giving up her rented studio flat and moving into Fran's, neither caring what the neighbours thought – who, in any case, had mainly changed from the milestone party attendees.

In her early fifties, Fran was offered early retirement as her school was due to close. She could have moved to another, including Beth's, along with some of the pupils, but she declined and finished up at the end of the next summer term. Beth resigned from her school too, in accordance with their long-conceived plan, and they realised their dream of buying a shop on the high street, to be converted into the "Book Ends" bookshop – not a very imaginative or catchy title but Fran and Beth felt it best represented their relationship both with books and each other.

It took four months to be reconstructed and decorated in their own style, including armchairs dotted about and softly played classical music exuding through speakers in the ceiling, and they loved every minute of the planning and execution. They had a grand opening, with drinks and nibbles, and an upcoming, local female author, who was keen for the exposure, cut the ribbon and cake.

They never for a moment doubted it would be a

success, though their confidence was partly based on the knowledge that they only needed to make enough profit to feed themselves and pay the bills. Their enthusiasm was also infectious, and they established a wide clientele in the town, being careful to stock both the recently published and old classics. The shop wasn't large, but they guaranteed to source anything a customer requested, usually within days.

Fran organised author talks in the shop and at other venues in town, and Beth arranged themed evenings, such as Murder Mystery, Fantasy, Comedy and Victorian Melodrama, particularly popular in the long winters, when people would come and chat about favourite authors and books and often buy a book recommended by someone else.

One year the two-floor flat above the shop came up for sale, and Fran and Beth snapped it up. They moved in, letting out Fran's flat, with the view either to sell hers and stay above the shop or extend the shop upstairs. They dithered about this for a while, even contemplating turning the upstairs into a tea room, but eventually concluded, Fran in her seventies now, that they didn't want or need the hassle of another commercial project.

Fran sold her flat, at a significant profit, and they completely renovated the space above the shop, including refitting kitchen and bathroom. Beth also redesigned the "garden", transforming the reasonably sized patch of wasteland into a mainly paved area surrounded by raised beds and installing a marquee in the summer months so they could hold events outside.

Their happiness was complete when they were approached by a middle-aged couple, soon to be married, who had, very appropriately, met at a Book Ends Romance evening, with a request to hold the ceremony in the garden, subject to successful application for the necessary council licence, all at their own expense, of course.

Today, Fran and Beth were deep in contemplation and discussion of the council leaflet about the shop window display competition while Stella, a student who helped out occasionally, dealt with customers.

"We could, of course," said Beth, "fill the window with Christmas-themed books, but we'd probably be doing that anyway, as per previous years, and the council will know that. We need something different and more eye-catching."

Fran was screwing up her face in concentration. Somewhere, in the back of her mind, there was the tiniest chink of light. If only she could remember exactly what that lady customer had said, the one with the silver hair, engaging eyes, expressive hands and baseball cap. She would have been about the same age as Beth, not that that had anything to do with it. Something about bookshops and buses and trains…

Slowly, the memory extracted itself from all the other detritus in Fran's brain. Beth looked at her quizzically as a broad smile dawned.

"I've got it. A female customer, you know the one who's always wearing a baseball cap if she doesn't have her cycle helmet on and buys a lot of children's books as well, once said to me that you don't pass bookshops. They pass you, like buses and trains, and you either choose to jump on them, in other words, go into the shop, or not. If you do, they take you on a journey."

"What a lovely saying, and so true! But how does that help us?"

"We're going to build a train of books in the window."

# 8

Councillor Jim Blakeney, sitting at his desk in the old, grey-stone offices in the middle of town, which also housed the library and citizens advice bureau, was already regretting his decision to agree with his assistant, Sylvia's, suggestion to hold the shop window display competition.

He had to admit to himself that it was really only because he'd had to decline her request, just a few days before, to take three, rather than the usual two, weeks off next spring. It was just too much to ask at the busiest time of year for financials, meetings, planning applications and town summer event preparations.

He could tell that she'd half expected the sorrowful, but nevertheless still negative, response, but that unconscious acknowledgement of her own folly in asking, and embarrassment at being refused, only served to increase her bad temper. She'd flounced out of the room and his next cup of coffee had been laced with salt, not sugar – too late, he'd already taken a large gulp, which then splattered the keyboard and documents on his desk. He could swear too that he heard muffled giggling outside his door as

Sylvia shared the prank with Joyce, Councillor Ajay Rao's assistant.

Sylvia had taken all the calls, of course, from the town's shop holders, asking questions about the requirements, prize money, etc., but she'd, either deliberately or otherwise, managed to confuse herself about some of the detail, so she'd had to interrupt him four times while callers were on her phone and then, without saying anything, booked a half-hour slot with him in the afternoon to cover more items before phoning others back. And this was just the first day the competition was public knowledge!

Even Sylvia's sister (Gwen, Gwyn?) had called, allegedly on behalf of a friend of a friend who had a shop on the high street; he'd overheard them on his way out to the gents'. Well, either that or it was a cover-up for a personal chat on council time and phone; Jim didn't quite stoop to imagining that it was another piece of Sylvia revenge, his imagination and perspicacity not stretching that far.

And now he also had a list, compiled by Sylvia and proudly and loudly deposited on his desk while he was on a video call regarding waste management. Numbered items relating to the competition, with deadline dates, filled the whole page, albeit 1.5 spaced for ease of reading and ticking off. She'd chosen to interrupt him again, rather than e-mailing the document as normal, but she said she thought she'd make it easier for him by printing it off. She would also arrange another half hour with him tomorrow to go through the points and agree who would do what.

As Jim clicked leave meeting at the end of his call, he looked down the list and audibly groaned. Was there really no way he could let her have those three weeks off in March? Maybe Joyce could be called on to help him out as that would also help her friend? That assumed Ajay would allow it, of course, and he would be just as busy as Jim. Even taking on some of Sylvia's duties himself might be better than this slow torture.

Outside, Sylvia was busy finding the most inconvenient time for him to spend thirty minutes with her the next day. She eventually settled on squeezing it in between a meeting with Councillor Jordan about recycling and a visit to the newly refurbished primary school. Councillor Blakeney didn't normally deal with education matters, but Councillor Rao had asked if he'd take his place as he didn't want to distract or embarrass his son, who attended the school, with his presence. She knew her boss relished any prospect of getting both out of the office and into the community.

She'd considered credible ways of cancelling the trip for him or getting another councillor to do it, but then diverted tactics to making the visit as rushed as it possibly could be by detaining him in the office beforehand with her meeting. What else could she do to make his day more painful? She could absent herself for when he returned from the school visit, with all the stacked-up calls that would have occurred in their absence. She quickly phoned her dentist and asked for an emergency appointment the next day. It was true that she'd detected a loose tooth that morning, but it wasn't giving her any trouble and she could easily have waited. Better to be safe than sorry though, especially with teeth. They could do it in the morning or afternoon?

"Late afternoon, please. Thank you."

Sylvia replaced the phone and sat back in her chair, feeling much better after that.

# 9

It wasn't until after Ellie arrived home, put her bike and helmet away, got inside, half-filled Alex's food bowl and refreshed his water while he wound himself round her legs, that she realised she'd completely forgotten to buy a present at the toy shop, the most time critical task for the day!

She declaimed her absent-mindedness to Alex who listened, impatiently and noisily, until she put the food bowl down. She was ashamed of being so easily distracted by the rearrangement of the shop window display and the discussion with Greg at the bike shop. She'd then also had an exhilarating ride along the shore, the cold air whipping round her ears and neck (time to get the balaclava out) and, typically, lost track of the time, so she was doubly annoyed with herself.

Greg had been delighted with her suggestion for the competition, a recreation of the scene from the film, *ET*, where the kids are flying on bikes in front of a full moon. Ellie had absolutely loved that film and watched it often with Simon, more for her gratification than his, weeping every time to his great mortification.

It was a classic, just as relevant today as it was in its time. Surely every child, even today, had seen or heard of it? Not particularly Christmassy, but a film with a really feel-good factor and all about families, friends and welcoming strangers, which is what Christmas is about, surely? Who knows, it might even spark a desire in child or adult to have a bike for Christmas. It shouldn't be difficult to replicate either, and Greg immediately said he would print off a copy of the scene from the internet and they should meet to discuss again when he had it. He was truly grateful for her input as he'd been struggling a bit that morning with post and customers, let alone ideas.

The post had been from Gizza. Another begging letter, basically, blaming Greg for all that had happened to him since the trial; he was obviously well informed of the success of Greg's shop even if he no longer lived in the area. Ashamed of their son's actions, half suspecting the truth (they'd immediately offered to pay for the repairs to Greg's bike) and having to deal with the backlash from Gizza's father's employers, his parents had moved the family away as soon as they could after his community service was done.

Mindful of his past and fearful of certain people catching up with him, Greg eschewed social media, so post was one of the few contact methods available to Gizza, and the shop was certainly easy to find online – that was the whole point after all. It was also the most efficacious. If he'd phoned or texted, Greg could simply ignore or block. It was far from easy to ignore what landed on your doormat, in bold black and white.

On top of which, the fact that Gizza had actually handwritten the thing, in shaky, spidery and badly spelt script, couldn't help but have its intended impact on Greg. He felt bad. Prison had been awful – he would only have wished it on Gizza, who'd got him there – but it had given him chances not available to Gizza. What if it had happened the other way round?

The letters had started about four months ago. Despite saying nothing to his parents, for fear of worrying them, Greg showed a couple to Ellie. The content was much the same, but the tone progressed from pally banter to wheedling whining, then barely concealed threats on his person and premises. Ellie had tentatively suggested showing them to the police but got the response she expected. His parents then? Greg said he would think about it, folded up the letters and put them in a drawer.

"Please do that, and also consider more security arrangements at home and here."

Greg did just that. Over the next few weeks he had his own CCTV installed, in addition to what already existed on the high street, both in front of, and behind, the shop. He had the alarm checked again, even though he had an annual maintenance contract, the engineer looking at him quizzically as though wondering what he was trying to keep hidden. At his flat, he had an alarm and electronic device fitted at front and back doors so he could see anyone out there, also censor lights in both places. The building was set back from the road so at least he wouldn't be woken every night by passing people. He felt better after that.

Then he thought long and hard about what to write and came up with the following:

*Gizza,*

*I'm not your mate and never have been, so* (he deleted the "please" as it sounded soft) *don't talk to me as though you are. It's because of your lies that I spent four years in prison while you got off with community service. I've shown your letters to a few people* (an exaggeration, but Greg hoped this would scare him more) *who've suggested I contact the police. I haven't done that, yet, but if I hear back from you again, I definitely will. I do, however, feel sorry for your pathetic self* (he'd thought of mentioning gratitude to his dad for giving him the job at the warehouse in the first place but decided that might just rile the son even more), *so I've transferred £500 to the bank account you named, and that will be it. You will not get any more and, remember, if you ask again, I will go straight to the police. I've kept your letters as evidence, and I know where you live* (maybe a slight counter threat would help too). *There's a word for what you're trying to do and it's a crime too – extortion.*
*Greg*

He didn't handwrite it, as Gizza had done, but typed it on his laptop, printed it off and signed it by hand, in a bid to give it additional formality and legitimacy, which might just scare Gizza a little bit more. *Best to be professional and detached*, he thought; this was a kind of business arrangement after all.

He didn't show the letter to Ellie, though he gave her the gist of what he'd written. He hadn't wanted her, or anyone else, to stop him. This was his problem, and he had to deal with it. She smiled and congratulated him on his quick decision-making and was very glad to hear about the increased security at the shop and his home, but he could see that she was still worried. He was doubly glad he hadn't told his parents; Ellie was always a slightly more detached and objective reflection of how they would react.

He then metaphorically sat back and waited for whatever would happen next to do just that.

# 10

Two days after Ellie's first meeting with Billy Anderson (she'd deliberately tortured herself, as punishment for her forgetfulness, by waiting another day, having checked first that she'd still be able to deliver the little girl's gift in time), she visited him again. As she cycled along the high street, checking the best place to leave her bike, she noticed a difference from last time: some of the shops had started to rearrange their window spaces, to begin to make way for, or experiment with, the display to be offered up for council inspection. This made Ellie wonder again, as she had a lot during the last two days, over her eerily clairvoyant idea to resuscitate Billy's window display, now the subject of comments from passers-by as she neared the shop.

Ellie was even more pleased to see a couple of customers inside. Billy looked over as the bell above the door jingled, smiled broadly and raised a hand in salutation; Ellie waved back and started browsing. The selection of younger children's games and puzzles was truly impressive, and Ellie enjoyed herself pulling some out to turn them over and read the instructions or just look at the pictures more closely. They were all clearly marked with which age range they were suitable for. By the time she'd spent a fun ten minutes doing this, Billy had finished with his earlier customers and walked over to her; he was practically skipping.

"It's been pretty busy since you were here last. Not everyone who's come in has bought something – they were just made curious by the windows – but if they didn't, almost everyone said what great stock I had and they'd definitely come back when they needed a youngster's present."

He was grinning unashamedly, showing remarkably good teeth for what must be his age.

"Now, you must let me get that cuppa for you. Tea or coffee? And I hope you won't think me really cheeky, but I've got another favour to ask you. Isn't it strange, about this council competition though? It made me wonder whether you're psychic, like people you see on TV. I only found out yesterday from my grandson. It was on social media too – that's where he spotted it. I don't do that sort of thing. Good that he keeps an eye open for me though. The young are so much better at technology, aren't they?"

Ellie smiled back, curious.

"I'm definitely not psychic, sorry to disappoint. I'll have tea, please. Milk, no sugar. Thank you. And I'd like to buy this, please."

It seemed they were already the best of friends and, after Ellie paid for and put away the puzzle, Billy took her through to the back of the shop where there was a tiny sitting area with an armchair and stool.

"I need to come through here from time to time to put my feet up. I can hear the bell fine from here. My daughter said I should see about getting a camera in the shop so I can watch from a TV screen in here – you know, in case of shoplifters – but I've never had any trouble like that and there are CCTV cameras along the street. Do you mind taking the stool? I'm really sorry, but if I got down on it myself, I'd have real trouble getting back up again, with these knees."

Ellie, laughing, said she'd be delighted and would have insisted on it anyway, and Billy busied himself with the kettle and teapot.

"If you don't mind me asking, why do you carry on with the shop if it's a lot of bother for you? You're surely well past retirement age?"

Billy chuckled, obviously delighted that she felt they were good enough friends for brutal honesty. As soon as Ellie heard her own words though, she blushed.

"Sorry, that sounded very cheeky, even rude, but it's more concern for you if you're struggling a bit."

A deeper blush as she seemed to have made the hole even bigger now.

Billy turned and offered a mug of tea, which he handed to Ellie, and a plate of biscuits, which he put on a table between the stool and armchair.

"You're absolutely right, I do struggle. But I think I'd be bored without it. I'm on my own at home, you see, and this is a way to talk to a lot of people. And I love seeing the new toys come in. They're so different to what they were in my day, but in many ways exactly the same, if you see what I mean?"

Ellie did, exactly and, now only a pinkish colour, sniffed her tea appreciatively and settled down for a chat.

"Talking of cheeky, which I was, what's the favour you want to ask me?"

"I've had a new train set come in. It's bound to be a good seller for Christmas. I was wondering if you could help me clear a bit of space at the back of the shop and set it out on a low table there so that even the smaller kiddies can see it. We could get it running from time to time too, by adding a timer. That's what my grandson, Andy, suggested. He felt bad he couldn't help but he's got mock exams coming up and needs to study. That's why he hasn't been in as much recently. He said he'd order a timer off the internet for me though."

"I'd love to do that. I've never really played with a train set before though, so you'll have to be in charge. It's something my son was never interested in. He preferred games to toys, especially the ones he knew he was good at and others weren't, so he could beat them."

"You'll know best where to put things though, you know, like people and trees and things. You're good at that sort of thing. I'll easily assemble the trains and get them working though."

Before sitting down, Billy almost bounced away and came back with a large box, which he gave Ellie while taking her mug and putting it on the table. She peered at it intently.

"Wow, this does look impressive. I had no idea! The trains look really authentic. And it's even got lights and makes sounds and smoke!"

Billy grinned again and rubbed his hands together.

It wasn't easy making a space big enough for the table but, once Ellie had carefully taken the ladder from its corner into the back room and they'd replaced it with some of the taller, narrower stands, it could just be managed. It had folding legs so was relatively easy to get into position and then upright. Billy had obviously been thinking about this for a while as he then disappeared into the back again and returned with a thin, green, baize cloth, which he spread across the table. Ellie smiled approvingly. They then set about emptying the box and assembling the trains, Billy clearing the counter as much as possible so he could stand there to connect the engines, carriages, freight wagons and tracks.

Customers came in from time to time, so Billy had to serve them, all the while excitedly telling them what they were doing and urging them to come back in the next few days to see the finished article. Some of them went to the back of the shop to look, where Ellie was busying herself with the trees, admired the intricacy of the pieces, studied the box and asked how easy it was to put together. Billy declaimed enthusiastically about the project while he showed them what he was doing at the counter.

It was well after lunchtime by the time they both realised how hungry they were, and they still weren't entirely satisfied with their work. Ellie offered to get something for them both from the deli and Billy agreed, as long as he could pay for it. He didn't say, but he'd actually brought his sandwiches with him, as usual, much preferring to have something with Ellie, and they'd be fine for the next day as he'd had the foresight to put them in their box in the cool just outside the back door.

After lunch and another cup of tea, they rearranged the track again. Ellie had discovered that some of the pieces were curved upwards and downwards, as well as from left to right, to allow the rails to go up- and downhill. She found a few items in the back room, after checking with Billy, and, carefully placing them underneath the baize, created various degrees of incline. Billy was sceptical, commenting that railway engineers would never build a track like that: the whole purpose was to go in a straight line and through a hill, if necessary, rather than over it. Ellie agreed but was sure she'd read in a book somewhere that they could go up and down on a special kind of rail. There was no evidence of that kind of rail in the train set, but Billy's customers weren't going to see that, were they? Billy's face brightened up again.

By the time Ellie had placed the last waiting passenger on the platform, holding a dog on a lead, run outside and added her final touches, Billy was ready to switch on. He was shuffling from side to side with anticipation, controller in hand. He clicked and the train started to move slowly. They had to adjust some of the track, following a few derailments on the first rotation, but eventually the train glided fairly smoothly over the baize. Billy chuckled heartily as he experimented with the smoke and whistle, and Ellie laughed too, though feeling regretful that Simon had never wanted a set. What fun they could have had together.

Billy suddenly handed the controller to Ellie and went to the counter, looking for his phone. He came back with it.

"Do you know how to take a video on this thing? I want to send it to someone. Andy says it can do it, but I've never needed to. Susan always likes my phone to be reasonably up to date so it doesn't go wrong, but it's got loads of stuff on it that I never use."

Ellie swapped it for the control and studied it. It wasn't that different from her own.

"Okay. You get the whistle and steam working again from time to time and I'll take a video of it going round a couple of times."

Afterwards, they laughed at the result and Ellie showed Billy how to find the recipient, create a message and attach the video. Well, more truthfully, she did it herself with him looking on and dictating. She couldn't resist asking, "Who's Chrissy?" with a sidelong glance, half hoping he'd betray a secret girlfriend.

Billy laughed.

"I know what you're thinking. I wish. She's the florist down the road. She's a lovely girl. She's not from the area, but I know her dad and try to keep an eye on her for him. I'm afraid she's in a wheelchair so it's quite difficult for her to visit my shop, though I would reorganise everything if she said she was coming in. As it is, I have to ask mothers to leave pushchairs outside – there just isn't space. What else can you do when these buildings are so old and protected so you can't change much?"

Billy watched, fascinated, as Ellie clicked send.

# 11

Chrissy had been busy with the table arrangement that morning and customers booking Christmas wreaths, having spotted the sign she'd added to the window first thing: "20% discount if ordered before the end of October. 50% deposit required". She'd calculated that having half the money upfront, and what she could do with it, would more than compensate for the price reduction; on top of which, getting as many orders in as early as she could meant she'd be able to negotiate a better price for the materials.

She'd phoned Dad last night too, who was always a good sounding board even when her mind was actually pretty much made up, and he'd been encouraging. He'd asked after Billy too, but Chrissy had to confess she hadn't seen him for a while. She immediately determined she'd give him a call later. Apart from anything else, she wanted to talk to him about the council window display competition. She hadn't said anything to Dad about it as she wanted some ideas first, which she could then talk through with him. She might even take a trip home so they could talk properly.

It was perplexing her more than just a bit. It wasn't easy for a florist to create something that would last for the period of time the leaflet she'd picked up earlier stated it needed to be available. It wasn't just one, or even a couple of days, during which the judging would take place; it had to be there for over three weeks, as part of the town's Advent celebration and to give everyone time to see them all. One of the aims of the competition, the leaflet expounded, was to encourage people to visit their local shops and use them: an admirable sentiment, Chrissy thought, if it had any chance of working. And the display, for her, had to be about floristry, as well as having a seasonal theme; she had to be selling the shop and what she could do. But she couldn't afford the expense or time of replacing fresh pieces over a three-week period.

Luckily, she was distracted by the customer coming in to collect the table decoration. She was so happy with Chrissy's work that she ordered two Christmas wreaths, which cheered Chrissy up considerably. The customer also commented on how exciting it was that the council was holding this shop window display competition and maybe it would really help local businesses; was she going to enter too? *Brave pants required here*, thought Chrissy, and, beaming widely, she said , "Of course! And it will outshine all the rest, wait and see."

Later, Chrissy wondered at her insanity and what had provoked it. *Probably, subconsciously, Maureen blooming Enderby*, she thought. Yes, she would do this and, if she could just beat that woman, who is bound to enter the competition, that would be more than enough satisfaction to last for her tenancy of the shop, whatever that might be.

Just then her phone pinged.

How funny, as she'd been thinking of him. She'd never got a text from Billy before, just brief phone calls or lengthier visits. Hold on, there was an attachment too. For a few seconds, Chrissy was thrown by Billy's unexpected technical ability until she read that *Ellie* (who's Ellie? she wondered) *took the video and helped me send this. Isn't it great?*

Chrissy had to agree that it was. Train sets were far from being her thing, but the playfulness of the vehicle travelling round, spouting smoke, over pretend grass; past pretend fields of pretend cattle, sheep and horses; up and down pretend hills, through pretend autumn trees and past pretend stations with pretend passengers waiting, fruitlessly, was captivating. For a moment she was mesmerised, transported into a world, long gone, of iron and steam, unspoiled pasture, trees and leaves.

Leaves. Someone had sprinkled tiny pieces of leaves over the whole creation so that the end result really was a beautiful autumn picture. Chrissy looked again, more closely now and pausing the picture from time to time. Someone had also painted orange, yellow and red spots on the branches of the green, plastic trees. They'd gone to a lot of trouble to create the autumn effect. And the scattered shreds of leaves were dry. It hadn't rained, but been dull and windy, for quite a while: dried, brown and golden leaves were gathered everywhere in town, blown against the shop walls and into the gutters. And also across the scene she was now seeing, revolving, on her phone.

A tiny thought entered her mind. Not even an idea, really. Dry leaves. She was expert at potpourri, loving the process, which was a bit like cooking but better. Her eyes moved slowly across the shop to one of the recycling bins she'd fed today. Yes, she could do this, and with very little extra expense.

Chrissy rolled round her shop in celebration.

"Maureen Enderby, I'm going to beat you!"

# 12

One of the first items on Sylvia's list, added to further torment him, Jim Blakeney thought grimly, was a get-together of all the shop holders who had entered the competition. Nothing fancy: just tea, coffee, soft drinks and biscuits in the council building conference room on a Wednesday afternoon when many of the shops were closed. It would be an opportunity, she told him, for the councillor to answer any last-minute questions as a one-off, rather than all the to-ing and fro-ing there'd been on the phone at the start, which would be much more convenient for him. She'd drafted a short introduction for him, which he could review and embellish, as he wished, and a list of what she thought might be asked, with appropriate responses. She would attend as well, of course, and every shop holder could bring one guest. Entries were looking promising but not overwhelming so the room would be plenty big enough.

Wednesday afternoon arrived, all too quickly. When everyone was assembled and standing round, nervously juggling saucers and biscuits, Sylvia walked to the top of the room, requested silence, introduced herself and told them that Councillor Blakeney would now say a few words. Then everyone could mingle again and approach him, or her, personally with any questions they still had about the competition, though she hoped it was all fairly clear by now. She reminded everyone to contact Councillor Blakeney, or herself, as soon as they had chosen the theme of their shop window display, and notify them of any changes that might happen afterwards; also, that they were to keep their plans as confidential as possible. These were both absolutely critical for the smooth running of the competition. Choices had to be made and communicated within (consulting her diary), well, actually, within three weeks of today. She would be visiting them personally to check the appropriateness (muffled chuckles from the audience) and progress of the displays and would, of course, give them adequate notice of this. She then heartily wished everyone the best of luck and smiled graciously round the room.

At which point the councillor joined her, cleared his throat, introduced himself, welcomed and thanked everyone and her, and then more or less repeated exactly what Sylvia had just said (trust her to pre-empt him so he looked stupid and redundant!).

Maureen was there, with Bridget as her guest. She was starting to regret inviting her now, wishing she'd dragged Frank along instead or feigned illness so that she wouldn't have to go herself either. But Frank was grumpy when she raised this possibility with him and curiosity got the better of her, so here they both were.

They spoke, with forced and exaggerated politeness, even affection, to each other, only when necessary. They were both well aware, having known each other since their schooldays, that if they were calling each other "dear", things were very bad between them. The source of the falling out was, of course, arguments about what Maureen's Christmas shop window display should look like.

Having been asked by Maureen for help, something that didn't often occur, Bridget was trying to take the upper hand, and Maureen wasn't having it. Consequently, every idea Bridget raised was quashed by Maureen, for one reason or another, none of which had validity in Bridget's eyes. Eventually, she'd stopped offering suggestions and then Maureen was in a stew because she couldn't materialise any ideas herself and became even crosser with her friend as a result. Maureen tried to distract herself, and isolate Bridget even more, by looking at the people in the room she was most interested in.

Billy was there, with his daughter, Susan. He looked across and raised a hand in acknowledgement. Susan smiled at her too. Maureen and Billy were the longest-serving shopkeepers in the town, and therefore should stick together, Maureen determined. She made a mental note to chat to him about his ideas for his windows, although they were already looking impressive.

The barber was there too, with his wife. Maureen had never really properly talked to them, so she stored away another mental note. His wife was gorgeously attired in a colourful trouser suit; trousers that gathered at the ankles to reveal beautiful, golden sandals and painted toenails below. Large, hooped earrings swung from her ears and her dark hair, with hardly a streak of silver, was piled high on her head, clasped by an intriguing creation of gold-coloured metal (surely it wasn't real gold, though she was dressed exotically enough for anything to be true), from which cascaded brightly coloured streaks of, what, silk? She made everyone else in the room look quite drab so that Maureen looked down, rather depressed, at her dull tweed and wool.

The barber was obviously very proud and protective of his wife as he listened intently to everything she said, laughing frequently, and rarely moved his hand away from lightly cradling her elbow (when had Frank ever done that to her?).

The bookshop owners, Fran and Beth, she knew reasonably well, having established contact by dropping in when they first opened the shop. She had been curious to know whether they were going to stock any items that could be construed as gifts; and she did sell books about the local area herself, after all, so there could be competition there. She came away reassured and full of the tea, cake and flattery they'd dished out to her. Fran and Beth instantly recognised a person they should stay on the right side of, and someone who was obviously a fountain of useful knowledge of local subjects, if quite obtuse about certain matters right under her nose. They gave, and Maureen jumped at, the impression they were old school colleagues, now both single (or was it widowed?), paid off from work and embarking together on an adventure they felt risky but which had to be tried. Therefore, they would be very grateful for any advice or knowledge Maureen could share with them as a long-standing shop holder, excuse me, huge apologies, shop owner.

When the door closed after Maureen, Fran and Beth could hardly control themselves with laughing, but they both admitted to a tinge of shame, feeling a bit sorry for the narrow-minded, old woman. Thereafter, Maureen did keep an eye on the bookshop, jealous of any deviation from their professed plan that day, but nothing had given her cause for concern. They exchanged tea, coffee, cake and chat from time to time at both premises, sometimes even with Frank present too, who enjoyed their lively banter, but even more their shameless teasing and flirting with him.

Fran and Beth waved vigorously across the room to Maureen, and she gesticulated accordingly in return. They weren't dressed at all exotically, unlike the barber's wife, though Fran's attire was certainly unconventional in its flowing, colourful folds, but there was a sense that the room paid unconscious homage to them. Their talk, even to each other, was so animated and they soon joined other groups, with ease, and other groups joined them. Maureen sighed, resignedly. She now painfully wished that Frank had come, as he'd have been over to join them like a shot, while she was stuck with boring, truculent old Bridget.

Greg and Ellie, his plus-one, were talking to Chrissy and Debbie. Greg had motioned them all over to the edge of the room so he and Ellie could sit on chairs and be on a level with the others.

"Saves us cricking our knees or you your necks," he said, and Chrissy and Debbie laughed.

"We've got the advantage over you though", responded Chrissy, "we've got a lap to store a plate of biscuits", and she offered them round to everyone.

Their laughter caught Billy's attention, and he turned to wave to them. They waved back and Chrissy blew him a kiss. Billy returned the favour and Susan laughed.

"My dad and Billy are old friends," Chrissy explained. "Billy's been helping me out since I arrived, though we've both been too busy recently to see each other. I must chat with him before I go as Dad was asking about him."

Turning to Ellie, she said, "That was a brilliant video you did for him. He sounded so excited in the background. Dad always said he was mad about train sets."

Berk and Defne were talking to Councillor Blakeney and his assistant, Ms Fellowes ("No, please call me Sylvia"). Berk was waxing lyrical about his clever daughter, Lola, Defne quietly putting a hand on her husband's arm and throwing sideways glances in an attempt to restrain him.

"She's coming home next weekend. We'll be so happy to see her again. It's such hard work, studying to be a doctor, you know. She works too hard. I worry about her."

At which point Sylvia achieved total, unassailable conquest over Councillor Jim Blakeney by reaching across and gently touching Berk's other arm.

"You're absolutely right to be concerned about your child, Mr Arsian."

Did she even have children? She'd never spoken about them. He had no idea, but then, why would he?

"There are a lot of mental health issues out there in young adults these days. They are all under so much pressure. All you can do is give unconditional love and support and wait patiently for them to come home to you."

At which, Berk and Defne melted, and Councillor Blakeney heartily wished he could sink through the hardwood council floor.

# 13

Greg very nearly missed his train home. He was tempted to jump on his bike as he ran along the platform with it, but the place was busy and he saw alarmed looks from passengers, which would have turned to horror, he knew, not to mention the opprobrium he'd receive from the groups of station staff. He found the carriage with the bike stand and launched himself, followed by the bike, onto it, breathing heavily and sweating slightly. He secured the bike, hung his helmet on the handlebar and collapsed, with relief, onto a seat with his rucksack on his lap. He dug into its depths before standing up and heaving it onto the rack above his head.

He'd been at his grandparents' place with his mum and dad for a few delicious days. They lived just outside a village in the Scottish Highlands, a house and place he'd always loved, and he'd spent many an amazing holiday there with them, either with his parents or alone, as he grew up. It was partly due to them that he found the straighter road again. They never judged or condemned, saying there was a reason for everything if you just took the time to look; and, when you'd found it, well, then you could do something about it, or at least understand.

The cycling had been awesome too: often alone but sometimes with Dad. He loved those excursions. He'd got Dad into cycling with him, just occasionally, as a teenager and, now Dad was semi-retired, he'd developed a real interest and often messaged Greg, with photos, about where he'd been.

This time, they'd headed off through trees, past lakes with pebbled shores and hills with craggy outcrops and waterfalls, crossing bridges spanning bubbling streams, a myriad of birds swooping crazily, and sometimes noisily, overhead. The sun was quite low now and it painted the sky with orange and azure streaks reflected in the water and backdropping the copper, red and yellow of the trees. The air bit through his balaclava and gloves but he loved the sensation and anticipated pleasure of warming face and hands in front of his grandparents' flaming and pine-smelling log fire. Dad had loved it too, putting his arm round Greg's shoulders as they started to push their bikes back up the track towards his grandparents' cottage, a beautifully extended, stone croft, smoke spiralling from its main chimney. His grandparents' black-and-white collie bounded towards them, barking ecstatically.

Later, after baths and chat about where they'd been and how the others had spent their day, they sat down to an immense meal of stew and dumplings, followed by Greg's grandmother's legendary apple pie. The table cleared and washing up done between them, they sat down again and played board games for most of the rest of the evening, his grandfather turning on the TV for the late news only, which was, of course, all bad.

Greg smiled to himself on the train. He'd been up there for three days in total but the last one, yesterday, was always the best. He was glad his mum and dad were staying for longer too as that was good company for his grandparents; it was always easier to leave them if they weren't going to be alone. Catching himself, Greg suddenly realised he'd been unintentionally staring and smiling at the young woman sitting opposite him for the last few minutes. She didn't seem to be offended and smiled back, quizzically, when she finally caught his eye. To cover his embarrassment, and because he really did intend to while away the long journey home reading his book, he opened it. It took him a few minutes to sense that she was now staring straight back at him; no, hold on, not him, his book. She moved the one sitting on her own lap so he could see the front page. *The Count of Monte Christo*. This was staggering. His own book was *The Three Musketeers* by the same author, Alexandre Dumas, recommended to him by Ellie. They both smiled again, this time more broadly, over the joke.

"Mine was given to me by my dad," she offered. "He'd heard from one of his customers, an older lady, I think, who'd been in to buy a gift voucher for her son, that it was very good. He's a barber, you see. He was asking his customers what they could recommend for me but, given they were all men, he decided to ignore their suggestions, which all sounded pretty poor anyway, and accept hers. I'm glad he did: it's a great book for taking my mind off studying, which is what he wanted it for. It's full of greed, jealousy, double crossing and revenge, but it's a love story as well. Loads of action and characters; it just kind of races along. And it's got some Turkish history in it."

"This one belongs to a friend who leant it to me," Greg responded. "I'm really enjoying it too. Sounds fairly similar to yours. What a coincidence."

There were more to come, starting with where they were both going. By this time, they'd exchanged books to read the other's synopsis on the back and talked about more favourite authors, some of which they had in common.

"Have you been to the bookshop in town?" she asked. "It's really good, I love it in there, and they'll order any book they don't have within days. I love Fran and Beth: they were great when I was ordering books for school."

Greg confessed he hadn't really as he only had time to read when he was away visiting family. He was too busy running his shop. That's why Ellie had given him the book; he hadn't even had time to think about what to bring for the journey.

"How funny that you have a shop too!" She was incredibly pretty when she became animated, Greg decided. Well, actually, incredibly pretty all the time, but he loved it when her dark eyes, with their fabulous, long, black lashes, stretched up– as well as outwards. "What is it?"

So, Greg told her all about it and how his foster parents and their parents had helped him. That's where he'd been the last few days, with them. They'd had a great time. Now it was time to get back to work. He had a busy time ahead, before Christmas. He always visited at this time as he knew he wouldn't see them again for a couple of months.

"No coincidence there; it's the opposite for me," she said. "I'm heading home for a bit of a rest, though I've brought some study books with me too. There's no let-up at this point on the course. My dad will make sure I do as little work as possible though."

"Hold on. Your dad isn't Berk Arsian, is he? I don't know him that well, but he has the shop along from me on the high street. I was talking to him just a few days ago, actually, at the get-together for the council shop window display competition."

He was pleased to have surprised her as those eyes expanded again.

"Yes, it's him. I'm his daughter, Lola. He told me about that. So, you're entering too. Do you know what you're going to do or is it a trade secret?"

They both laughed at that.

"Not exactly, but we were told at the council meeting to keep it to ourselves. I think they're trying to increase the suspense, and they're worried about our plans getting out to the public, where they want everything to be a total surprise. We have to share them with the council first though. You know, to make sure it's all appropriate and there's no duplication. I'm Greg Murphy, by the way. Nice to meet you, Lola Arsian."

Lola responded likewise and they shook hands.

Before they got off the train at their destination, Lola insisting on helping Greg with his bike, they'd exchanged phone numbers and agreed to meet for coffee in town while Lola was at home.

# 14

In addition to awarding Sylvia what she considered to be total victory over her boss, Councillor Jim Blakeney, the meeting at the council buildings also watered a germ of friendliness, even camaraderie, among the town shopkeepers. It was stunted, of course, by a tinge of jealous competitiveness in some, usually acknowledged and brushed aside, humorously.

Maureen and Billy could be seen drinking coffee together frequently in either shop; she suddenly, to Frank's bewilderment, given frequent attacks on his sweet tooth, discovered a desire to bake, such that she was often seen trotting up and down the high street with small plastic boxes she generously distributed, even to Chrissy Dickson. The latter gift was bestowed with an affected consideration, which Chrissy found nauseatingly patronising, though she accepted it, graciously, and later deposited the contents of the box in the bin.

Greg took the opportunity of his few words with Berk at the event to walk along to the barber's shop one morning and book himself an appointment for just before Christmas to give himself a much-needed tidy-up before he met his family then. He dropped into the conversation that he'd met Lola on the train, and Berk acknowledged that he'd heard the same from her. He looked at Greg out of the corner of his eye, quizzically but not completely disapprovingly. Greg tried not to look shifty. He just didn't want to see Lola again without her parents being aware they were friends (and becoming more, if he could possibly manage it).

Fran and Beth generously offered tickets to all bookshop events from then until Christmas to local shop holders for free. These events became rather frivolous, and sometimes slightly tipsy, get-togethers after the usual literary guests had left, both women revelling in their merciless teasing of all their neighbours about possible window display themes.

They speculated that Billy would abandon the window space to electronic gaming equipment of all descriptions; Greg would fill it with tandems and penny farthings; Maureen would satisfy a long-held desire to show an array of the usual lewd Christmas gifts associated with office Secret Santas; Berk would have a mechanised belly dancer, accompanied by flautist, violinist and drummer; and Chrissy would show a full demonstration of the cultivation of marijuana.

To their noisy and amused delight, Chrissy immediately riposted that Beth and Fran would no doubt fill the windows with books of Victorian pornography dug out of the basement, where she was confident only elite, and very respectable, male customers, such as Councillor Blakeney, were normally granted access. "That is a good idea!" from Beth, once they'd all recovered. "I've often thought of converting the cellar. We're lucky enough even to have access from the back, like some of the other shops on the street. A perfect and very discreet entrance for our dodgier clients!"

To Greg's delight, Lola attended one of these bookshop events with her father while she was home. She'd told Berk she wanted the chance to meet Fran and Beth properly again, after all those years they'd helped her at school. She did indeed monopolise them for about twenty minutes, during which time Berk stood aside, beaming, while he watched the bookshop owners declaiming about his daughter's appearance, wrapping Lola in their arms in turn and later locking heads with her in gossipy catch-up, interspersed with giggles and snatches of laughter. Between this and Berk's insistence that he introduce his daughter to every person in the room, so he could tell them how clever she was and what she was doing, Lola had no time to spare for Greg, though she did strain her eyes across the room from time to time, trying to see where he was. Greg in turn tried to catch her eye every ten minutes, but it seemed every time he did, she was fully engaged with someone else.

They did manage to catch a few minutes with each other when the group split up and Berk went to the toilet. They felt quite conspiratorial.

"You didn't say yesterday you were coming," from Greg.

"It was a last-minute thing. Mum was going to come but I overrode her as it was my only chance."

Was Greg just dreaming, probably yes, or did she look just a bit, well, coquettish? The lashes were up, beautiful dark eyes looking at him intently, and then down, secretively, the corners of that lovely mouth curling upwards deliciously.

Greg almost gulped.

"Well, it's great to see you, even if just for a few minutes. I thought it would be ages until the next time."

"So did I."

Greg spotted Berk starting to walk across the room.

"Stay in touch, eh? I love hearing from you."

"Me too. I will, don't worry."

Greg almost danced out of the room. Not only had that happened, but he'd had lunch with Lola the day before, although it hadn't begun very propitiously. He'd suggested a place on the high street, which did amazing soup and all kinds of exotic sandwiches and rolls and was close to the bike shop, as he had an appointment at 2.00. Greg had told Lola then of the forthcoming bookshop event, but she hadn't said anything about accompanying her dad

Conversation had been excruciatingly stilted at first, at least from Greg, after the surprise and informality of their chance encounter on the train; he silently but vigorously upbraided himself for wanting the meeting to go so well that he was afraid of saying the wrong thing and therefore ran out of things to say almost entirely. Lola seemed more at ease, particularly when he asked her about her studies, student accommodation and friends, and she complimented his choice of venue as the soup and coffee were really good.

The mood did lighten when they talked about the books they were reading, then, very unsubtly, tried to interrogate each other about respective window displays. This led on to speculation, not quite as cheeky as Fran's and Beth's the following day, about other shops. Lola also asked him how the cycle shop was doing and what plans he had for the prize money if he won. He told her vaguely of his intention to expand, almost afraid to articulate his ideas in the face of the unlikelihood of being able to realise them, but her rapt attention was soothing and encouraging. She had no notion of what her father was planning to do with any winnings. They then tried to guess, jokingly, about what other shopkeepers might do.

Time flew, until Lola reminded Greg that he'd said he needed to be back at the shop by 2.00. Then there was the awkwardness of Greg insisting on paying the whole bill himself, since it had been his idea to meet, which Lola finally accepted on the proviso that she would return the favour when she was back for the Christmas holidays, at which Greg's eyes visibly lit up.

The next dilemma was how to say goodbye outside the shop. He was unlikely to see her again before she returned to university. Should he shake her hand (no, too formal); should he just wave obliquely as he disappeared into the distance (no, too casual). Lola took matters into her own hands by smiling up at him, wishing him luck with the competition, and saying that they must make a date for that return lunch. She would message him with the dates of her next visit, and he should name the day as she could be flexible.

"I can't wait to see all the window displays as well. It makes coming home even more exciting than usual."

Greg said he couldn't wait for that time either. Then they did separate, slowly, and Greg turned back just before he knew Lola would be out of sight to find her doing exactly the same. Then they did both wave at the same time, together.

# 15

Harry Anderson drained his cup of Omani coffee (which he always thought tasted more like tea but was no less deliciously reviving for it), carefully placed the cup on the table in the hotel lobby next to the smoking frankincense burner, flung his rucksack over his right-hand shoulder, bowed in return to the two mahogany-skinned, smiling, dish-dash-wearing men guarding the automatic doors and passed, silently, through to the outside.

Immediately his sunglasses fogged over so, as usual, he took them off to wait for them to clear, while the hotel car curved smoothly round in front of the building to pull up alongside him. He smiled and gestured to the driver, as usual, that he could get into the car by himself, opened the rear passenger-side door, heaved the rucksack in after him and closed the door. The aircon immediately blasted deliciously cool air round the cab, making Harry shiver slightly from the contrast. It was only 6.30 in the morning, but Harry knew it was going to be yet another very warm and unseasonably humid day.

Harry never failed to make the journey to the construction site without marvelling at the determination of a people battling over the years against a harshly hot and dry climate; an absurdly rocky and arid landscape in this region; limited education and opportunities, particularly for women, despite plentiful resources, and incursion, welcome or not, from Western foreigners, Brits among them (*including him*, he thought wryly).

But, over the years Harry had spent there, the political and economic landscape had changed, with a more liberal sultan leading the charge to wrest the country from its own backwardness, just as he'd wrested power from his own father, and hacking an internationally acknowledged identity from it, just as contractors, such as Harry himself, literally blew and hacked spaces through and over mountains for roads and other infrastructure.

From time to time, as the car skirted the rugged coastline, Harry could discern where the rock formation of the cliff to left and right of the road changed from natural pocking and seaming, which resembled a honeycomb, to smooth concrete, where passage had been forced and the mountain shored up. Other evidence of Omani ingenuity was the capping of some mountains for access and the resulting rock deposits dumped along the coast to protect new shoreline developments from the battering of the sea.

As the car sped along wide, sweeping roads that almost tipped off the edge of the cliff and ascended and descended far into the distance, like a giant, concrete roller coaster, Harry loved to look at the craggy rocks and sheer escarpments to the right that just about prevented that accident from happening. Here and there, buildings had been sunk into the rocky outcrops between road and cliff: mainly large and expensive residential developments, but some small and plain, with decent-sized backyards and a patch they could call their own; all plainly and simply built from local stone, in keeping with, and no higher than, any surrounding, older buildings.

Nearer to the city centre, date palm trees and jasmine bushes lined the roads and Harry viewed appreciatively the new buildings behind them: schools, nurseries (very progressive, to allow Muslim mothers to work), hospitals, centres for medical, dental and (sadly) cosmetic surgery, the beautiful and imposing Royal Opera House Harry had seen being built over the years (a friend had been responsible for installing the lighting there), the even more iconic (just as it should be) four- or five-storey high Children's Public Library ("Knowledge Is Our Right") and the new university, where Harry was sure he'd read that the proportion of female students had recently started to outnumber males.

The gardeners, some female, were also busy at work in the "cool" part of the day, climbing palm trees to strip off dead leaves, sweeping up debris and rearranging sprinklers. Later, he knew, they'd be taking their lunch and a nap on mats spread under any available tree shade. Harry studied the flags fluttering high on building tops: not just of Oman and other Gulf and Arab nations. *Enemy to no one, friend to all. Not a bad philosophy for a country to have, at least as a starting point*, he thought.

Despite the new shopping malls, housing Carrefour,

McDonald's, IKEA, Starbucks and the like, Harry loved this place, its people and the way it had developed. Who could blame them for desiring the ease and pleasures of life that blossoming contact with the Western world could bring, as well as its own beloved religion and culture (as long as *they* don't change too much)? He thought they'd handled the balance pretty well, overall, if his taxi-driver friend, Asif, were anything to go by.

They passed the Nesto supermarket where Harry had spent many an evening provisioning for his rented apartment in the city centre. He'd loved that place, with its small but comfortable balcony where he'd sat eating a variety of Western and Arabic ready-made meals. His company had a very neat arrangement with a local hotel to enable procurement of alcohol for its, now relatively few, Western workers, so Harry could even enjoy the occasional beer or glass of wine on a Friday or Saturday evening. Asif had been over a few times and Harry had visited the souk to buy spices to attempt some Arabic dish, which Asif tolerated and laughed over. Somehow, Harry took this as a compliment because at least he did eat it (he joined Asif in drinking just water and coffee on those occasions). Asif would talk about his country and religion; Harry mainly listened as he couldn't comment much on his own, having not lived there for so long, though he did buy the occasional British newspaper to catch up on major events, not being much of a social media user.

A restless boy from his toddler years, he'd insisted on leaving home at sixteen, much to his father Billy's dismay and concern, to join the Merchant Navy; passed his Officer Cadet exams; then, fearing there was no long-term future in the service, obtained an apprenticeship in a construction company, slogging it up to degree level. He wasn't at all academic but loved to learn about the materials and machinery used in the industry and how they could be made to work together best; he also learnt how to deal with people to ensure that that happened with them too. Respectful of the fact that Harry had worked his way up from the bottom, and really did have a gift for the business, he was highly thought of and sought after in many of the company's major projects in the Middle East. Harry could be relied upon, they knew, not to offend either the local workforce or the authorities and was promoted accordingly.

Sadly, when the contract on the apartment came up for renewal, and the job still wasn't finished, having been plagued with supply issues (not Harry's fault), the company had chosen to let it lapse and move Harry into a hotel. Having employed him for so long, they knew full well there was a greater risk of Harry becoming complacent in his own place than in the impersonal and more controlling environment of a hotel. *Easier to keep an eye on me too*, he thought ruefully, after being told of the decision. He didn't mind that much. He'd already decided he was going to leave the company in about a year's time, when he would be just short of fifty-six years old. He did, however, regret not seeing Asif every day as he took him to and from site, and it certainly wasn't anywhere near as enjoyable entertaining him at the hotel.

This morning, he was carrying his resignation letter in his rucksack. Six months' notice was required, and he'd already verbally indicated to his boss that he wanted to return to the UK. "Wanted" wasn't exactly the right term though. Felt as though he had no choice was probably nearer the mark. He couldn't stay here forever, and the longer he delayed the decision, the more difficult it became. He'd discussed it with Asif at their last meeting, who'd advised Harry to act soon. His assumption was that Harry wanted to return to his family but even this wasn't entirely accurate. He did feel guilty, yes, about having abandoned them for so long, despite brief visits to the UK every two or three years, including to attend his mum's funeral, meet his nephew, Andy, for the first time and try to shore up Susan, with his dad's help, after her marriage broke down. Neither was it because he was feeling his age and wanted to take it easier now; if anything, the job kept him feeling fit and active. It was more that he was feeling the lack of roots: he'd never even had a mortgage, as accommodation always came with the current job, let alone a serious or long-term relationship with a woman, though they'd come and gone over the years with their own temporary working arrangements. If he were honest, that's how he'd liked it.

But now, here he was, a man approaching retirement age, with nothing much to show for it except an extremely healthy bank balance that wasn't working very hard for him. He needed somewhere to live in the UK, and why not make it somewhere not too far away from his family, particularly as Dad would start to need more help and it wasn't fair on Susan for her to keep providing it alone, particularly now she was on her own.

There was such a big age gap between him and his sister that he felt as though he'd hardly known her when he left home. Harry's mum and dad had been more or less kids themselves when Harry was born, and they'd both worried that the late arrival of his sister was one of the reasons for him leaving. Harry assured them otherwise. He just wanted to travel and experience other cultures

They certainly couldn't complain that he hadn't achieved his aim. Thank goodness for e-mail. Phone calls and post from the Middle East were seriously frustrating in the early days, although occasional calls absolutely required, particularly during Mum's illness and Susan's troubles. The struggle to conceive appeared to be in the family genes, as Susan waited years to fall pregnant with Andy. He was born on 30 November, to everyone's huge relief: so huge that his mother determined to call him Andrew despite his last name. The adjustment to parenthood was too much for Andy's father to take, however, and he left them both when Andy was a toddler. For once in his life, Harry had felt almost grateful that his mother wasn't there to witness her daughter's wailing grief and then, almost more painful for Billy and him, halting, stumbling but determined struggle to recover for her son's sake.

Yes, there was little doubt that Harry was needed at home, though the family had managed to come through without him. He was realistic enough to know there could be resentment that he'd left it so long and not been there when it really counted, but he sensed this might even help to make him feel better, like some kind of self-flagellation.

He'd give his boss the letter first thing, look at flights to make a prolonged (God knows, he had plenty of leave to take) visit to the UK around Christmas to give the family his news and visit the souk late afternoon to buy presents. What on earth would a teenager like Andy want? Maybe the mall would be better for him, with all those high-end, shiny shops selling electronics and the like. That would make a nice dent in his bank balance, at any rate.

Harry settled back into his seat. It was good to have a plan.

# 16

Gizza's immediate reaction on receiving Greg's letter was one of triumph. He'd made Greg pay up at last, and more than he was expecting, even though it was claimed to be a one-off. Never mind, he had it in his hands now. He was conscious of the underlying threats, of course, but chose to ignore them for the time being.

Gizza and his family had settled reasonably well at first into life in the large town they'd moved to down south. His dad got a transfer with the warehouse company; he got the distinct impression his boss had been glad to see the back of him, after all the flack he'd taken from the powers that be as a result of the boys' fight. They rented for a while, until the house at home was sold and they had worked out whereabouts they wanted to be. The new house was smaller, but his parents were pleased as it was newer and lower maintenance, with a much smaller garden. They were determined to make a clean start of it and encouraged Gizza to be positive about his prospects there.

The school was also better, though Gizza did struggle

to fit in for a while. It was difficult to make friends when everyone else already knew each other and they wanted to ask about his past and what had brought him to the area. Then he struck upon the idea of saying it was because of his dad's work, and it started to get a bit easier. He was still an outsider and not fully accepted, but this actually suited him to start with as he was happy to maintain his distance.

He'd also been largely clean from drugs since the trial, mainly due to the supervision he'd received and this being one of the judge's criteria for awarding community service only. His parents had made him promise too, as a condition for giving him their total support and removing him from the "mates" he claimed had led him astray. It suited them all to believe what they wanted to believe as they embarked on a new chapter together. They were all even invigorated by the change, Gizza's mum throwing herself into redesigning the house and garden and finding a part-time job for herself.

Gizza even began to enjoy school and achieve decent grades. His mum and dad were ecstatic; they'd known all along that the move was the best thing that ever happened to them. He applied, and was accepted for, a local electrician's apprenticeship. He worked hard and was qualified within three years. The company took him on, and he did well, becoming a favourite of the older female clients, with whom he flirted unashamedly and was therefore offered copious amounts of tea and homemade cake in between bouts of working.

Then, some years later, a previous colleague of Gizza's

dad transferred to the same site. Word quickly got round about the real reason for the family's move. Slowly but surely, his dad was made to feel uncomfortable at work and given the more unpleasant jobs to do. His boss became very short with him and picked him up at every available opportunity. Gizza's dad carried on, uncomplainingly, until one day when his boss called him into his office.

Citing the fact that the company was a very family-orientated one that prided itself on its values and those of its employees, he noted, as if in passing, that Gizza's dad had never been formally disciplined after what had happened at his previous employment: including allowing his own son onto the premises, a potentially dangerous place for unauthorised persons to be in the best of circumstances, let alone in the drugged-up state he was in, to then have a knife fight with another boy whom Gizza's dad had himself recruited. Gizza's dad's boss was now availing himself of the right to discipline him in the way it should have happened before, an omission that no doubt occurred in his previous boss's haste to be rid of him from his own site. He would pay him three months' salary (generous, as it could have been one, or even less) and he was to leave the warehouse that day.

Gizza's dad was stunned but probably not greatly surprised, given his treatment over the last few months, which he hadn't shared with anyone at home for fear of bursting everyone's bubble.

But now he had to go home and tell his wife and Gizza when he returned from work. He gathered his things and shuffled out of the building, suddenly feeling as though his legs were made of lead and he had to concentrate and work hard to move them, rather than them carrying him.

He stumbled a few times with the effort, provoking curious, and sometimes disapproving, looks from passers-by, some of whom assumed he was drunk. He started to sweat profusely and had to stop to wipe his forehead. Someone even stopped and asked if he was unwell, but he just mumbled a negative under his breath and shuffled on. Eventually, he came to the crossroads with traffic lights just a few hundred metres from home. Breathing heavily, he pushed the button to cross the road. In his eagerness to get across, he stepped out as soon as he saw the lights for traffic switch to amber in preparation for a pedestrian signal to cross.

He didn't stand a chance when the car speeded up to fly through the amber light before it turned red. Thankfully, neither did he see the car coming, or he would undoubtedly have frozen in horror and the collision would have been even worse. As it was, the corner of the car bonnet catapulted him across the other half of the road until he stopped in an ugly, distorted heap in the gutter. The car collided with a parked vehicle and came to rest, people running from all directions to both Gizza's dad and the driver.

It wasn't until after several months of his dad being in hospital, undergoing extensive and complicated surgery, that Gizza took out Greg's letter again. He'd already given his mum what was left of Greg's money, telling her it was a bonus from work. She didn't even bother to protest, his dad's salary having long stopped. The company had also offered an additional settlement, which she hadn't quibbled to accept immediately, in shock both from the accident and the news that her husband had been sacked on the day it happened. It was all just too much to take in, and Gizza saw her visibly shrink in front of his eyes over the months following the accident, from a positive, loving, competent woman to a weeping shadow who generally forgot to feed Gizza or herself, shunned all company and spent hours staring vacantly at nothing, when she wasn't sitting by Gizza's dad's side for hours on end at the hospital, speaking incoherently to him in his mainly comatose state.

Rage against his dad's company, and a paralysing but suffocated guilt over the reason for his dismissal, were commuted to rage against Greg in Gizza's befuddled mind. He read the letter again and again and decided that this awful state of affairs was entirely due to Greg. He'd pushed Gizza to do it, hadn't he? If it weren't for Greg, none of this would have happened. Sneaky, dirty little tike, worming his way into his dad's affections: that's what had really riled Gizza and forced him to retaliate. And now, because of that, his dad was lying in a hospital bed, unconscious and possibly never going to be conscious again. And his mum knew it – that's what was killing her too. And there would soon be no money, apart from what Gizza himself could bring home and the pitiful proceeds of a small insurance policy his dad had taken out several years ago. Gizza's dreams of saving up a deposit for his own place, so he could at last get out from under his parents' feet (not that they wanted that, but he certainly did), were shattered. And all the while Greg was rolling in it. If he wasn't, how could he have afforded to send Gizza so much money without a second's thought? Greg had destroyed his family and everything they'd achieved since they moved so far away solely to get away from him. They were suffering, so he should too.

Gizza had been hot-headed before, but he wouldn't be now. Greg should be made to pay for it. He *would* pay for it.

# 17

Ellie was now regularly spending time with Billy in his shop, on the pretext of Christmas shopping for young ones but also drinking a lot of tea and eating copious amounts of biscuits and (Maureen's) cake. She even felt guilty enough to contribute some herself, very apologetically as she'd never enjoyed, or been very good at, baking. They talked about new stock arriving for the shop, Billy excitedly showing Ellie his catalogues, supplier's pages on his laptop and printed pictures from Andy. They spent a lot of time mulling over the theme for the Christmas window display, feeling the pressure of having created a rather good one already. Ellie had several ideas but none of them really hit the mark, she felt. Looking round the shop, mug of tea in hand, helped her creative processes, she said, another good reason for popping in from time to time. The truth was that they enjoyed each other's company and conversation and were both quite lonely, though neither would have admitted to the latter.

Billy even spoke to her about his wife, Jeannie, a

rare occurrence for him with anyone. Ellie felt flattered, honoured, moved and slightly overawed. They'd met early on at high school, Billy told her. He was an awkward, painfully shy and self-conscious boy; Jeannie was the wild one of the class (maybe that's where their son, Harry, who was working abroad, got his restless nature from), whom boys were desperate to impress and girls' mothers warned their daughters away from. She dyed her flaming red hair black and got into all kinds of trouble for skipping school, not doing her homework, fighting in the playground and disrupting the class. Billy thought she was wonderful but, unlike any of the other boys, never plucked up the courage to speak to her.

Then one morning, Billy found an apparently abandoned kitten on the path on his way to school. He couldn't take it home as there would be no one to care for it there, his mum being out all day at the cleaning jobs she did, so he very tenderly tucked it into his satchel, carefully wrapping its warm, fluffy, tabby fur in his school scarf. It must only just have been left, or had perhaps escaped from someone's house, as it looked healthy enough. Its constant, high-pitched miaowing turned Billy's heart inside out.

Jeannie immediately spotted him stroking and talking to the kitten inside his satchel in the school playground and walked over, curious.

"What's in your satchel, Billy?"

Billy silently held the bag out to her so she could look inside. The kitten's big yellow eyes were all she could really see, but she could hear the mewling well enough.

"Oh, Billy, it's so tiny and cute! What are you going to

do with it?" she asked, quickly looking over her shoulder round the playground to check that no one else had noticed.

"I'll have to keep it here for today and see if I can find out who it belongs to later, though it looked as though it had just been left in the street."

"I'll help you look after it today. It's probably hungry and thirsty. We can give it some of our milk this morning. What shall we call it?"

Neither of them could tell whether it was a boy or girl. Billy peered down at it in his bag thoughtfully, his face scrunched up in concentration. Then he slowly looked up at Jeannie's face, her skin pale and translucent, those greenish eyes with their light auburn lashes, her perfect cheeks, nose and chin.

"Freckle."

Jeannie laughed so loudly that other kids did look round at them then, but they covered it up by pretending Billy had just told her a joke, something he was actually almost physically incapable of doing, successfully anyway.

They managed to conceal the tiny creature all day, Jeannie interrupting the class even more noisily than usual to cause a distraction whenever its pitiful cries threatened exposure. It slept a lot of the time, particularly after Billy and Jeannie painstakingly let it lick milk off their fingers in the morning and afternoon. It was too young to take any of the solid food they offered it from their lunchboxes.

At the end of the last break, just after the teacher had come out to the playground to ring the bell, Billy summoned all the courage he possessed and grabbed Jeannie's arm just as the children were forming a procession to return inside. He pulled her to the back of the queue to give them a bit more time.

"Can you come home with me tonight? I want Mum and Dad to let me keep it if we don't find out who it belongs to, and you can help me persuade them."

Jeannie opened her eyes wide in pleasure and excitement. "That's a great idea, Billy! I can tell them I'll help you with it. We can look after it together."

So, that's how it all started. Billy's parents were so surprised and pleased that he'd made a friend at school at last that they said yes as soon as both children offered up their pocket money to help pay for Freckle's keep. Billy's mum smiled kindly and thanked them both but said that wouldn't be necessary, at least for now. Billy and Jeannie did, however, combine their hard-earned pennies to buy some human infant formula milk, which Billy decided would be better for Freckle than what they had at home or school.

To Billy's and Jeannie's delight and relief, no one came forward to claim their pet, despite his mum and dad knocking on the doors of the houses near to where it was found. No one even knew of anyone whose cat had recently had kittens. It appeared that someone might even have driven there and dropped it off so as to remain anonymous. The children went to Billy's house at every break and lunchtime, Billy's parents having written a letter to the headteacher to explain why, to give the kitten milk from a tiny plastic bottle that Billy's mum gave them.

Freckle, a boy, thrived in Billy's and Jeannie's care, and

Jeannie took every opportunity she could to go and visit them both. They seemed to have a calming influence on her too, to her parents' and teachers' intense relief. She started to settle down to her studies and behave less rebelliously, though she would still have her moments, to the boys' (particularly Billy's) delight and girls' and teachers' horror. Billy grew more confident and less shy too, as he basked in Jeannie's attention and the other boys' envy.

As Billy's birthday approached, Jeannie asked him what she could get for him that he really wanted so she could start saving.

"You could buy me a new collar for Freckle." And then, looking at her closely, "Oh, and I want to see the real colour of your hair."

They were virtually inseparable after that. Neither of them left school with any qualifications, but it didn't seem to matter as Billy's dad had been left a greengrocer's shop in an elderly relative's will. Billy's parents were going to give up their current jobs to run it and Billy would work there too. When they left school in their late teens, Jeannie was already two months pregnant. They were married the following week. Jeannie moved in with Billy, his parents and Freckle and joined the family to work in the shop.

They all four loved it, learning the business and making mistakes along the way. Not long after Harry was born – a big bruiser of a baby who no one believed for a second was premature, but all the Andersons were delighted so what did it matter – Billy, Jeannie, Harry and Freckle moved into the rented flat above the shop. This really helped with running it and caring for Harry at the same time, Jeannie dashing up the stairs when he started to howl with hunger to feed him, and later bringing him down in his bouncy chair placed on the counter so he could stare at all the customers and they could make a fuss of him.

It continued much like this for many years, the family rarely taking more than a few days' holiday at a time here and there in the quieter times for the shop but enjoying spells by the seaside once Billy and Jeannie had saved enough to buy their own car. The whole family crammed into it to enjoy these excursions, an excited Harry squeezed between grandparents at the back (he loved to see the sea and had announced some time ago that he wanted to be a sailor when he grew up), all singing songs as they bowled along narrow country roads, peering hard through the windows to catch the sea in the distance as they neared their destination.

Billy and Jeannie gradually took over more of the strain of the shop as Billy's parents grew older, less healthy and mobile. Eventually, especially as it started to appear that their son and daughter-in-law would have no more children, they decided to retire and leave the business to them.

Billy and Jeannie were delighted, flattered and grateful, but the business wasn't succeeding as well now as it had in previous years. Supermarkets had started to pop up everywhere and people wanted to buy all their goods in one place. Billy had been pondering something for a long time but not yet even broached it with Jeannie.

About a week after his parents' retirement, he did. He wanted to turn the greengrocer's shop into a toy shop.

He'd been mulling it over for a long time, worked up some numbers and done his research. He thought it could be a real success. He showed everything to Jeannie, who started to buzz with excitement and hugged and kissed him in gratitude and anticipation.

The new toy shop, which emerged some months later, was like a talisman. Not only did it really take off, but it was only about a year after it was launched that Susan was born. Whether it was the adrenalin created by the change and its success or that Billy and Jeannie had more time for each other now, with Harry at high school, the ecstatic couple could only speculate. In time they would give up the flat above the shop and buy a house, as they needed more room. That's where Billy still lived.

Then Billy told Ellie about Jeannie's long illness and passing. His voice started to quake as he described his wife's initial tiredness, loss of appetite and weight, the diagnosis, the innumerable and lengthening spells at the hospital, the loss of her gorgeous, now silver-auburn hair, the stabbing, chokingly agonising and constant feeling of guilt that he could have done something to prevent it, that it was somehow his fault that she had to go through that almost unbearable agony. Jeannie hadn't given up; she'd fought valiantly, for his sake and that of the kids mainly, he thought – God knows, he was sure she'd have succumbed long before that without their futures to worry about, who wouldn't? – but that seemed only to prolong the illness, treatment and pain. She even managed to outlive Freckle, who died a very happy, cosseted and long-lived cat. They'd sat, hugging each other, rocking and crying on the sofa at home after it happened, both feeling that it was a bad omen.

She'd been a shadow of herself when she passed, and Billy knew that he'd lost his Jeannie, his real Jeannie, some time before. At least Harry managed to be home for the end; Billy liked to think that his wife was aware of their son's, in fact everyone's, presence at her bedside, though it seemed crazy, given the amount of medication they'd given her. It was actually almost a relief for them all when she slipped away; he was sure that's how they'd all felt, although no one said anything. No more pain or having to watch her endure it.

It was probably hardest for Susan, losing her mum as a teenager. Billy sometimes wondered whether the tragedy had made her vulnerable, so that she immediately flew into the arms of the most worthless young man Billy had ever met. At least she was free of him now and good riddance. "You never stop worrying about your kids, do you?", he said. Ellie laid a hand gently on his arm as they sat, drinking tea, at the back of the shop.

One day, Ellie paused longer than usual, mug in hand, over the train display they'd set out in the shop. Billy said that sales had been good – much better than last year – but not as high as he'd hoped. Ellie asked about more sophisticated sets, that adults might be interested in, as the one they'd set out was really for younger kids. Did he stock those? He hadn't before, Billy confessed. They went back to the laptop and browsed a few sites again, Billy getting quite excited about what he saw. These were not the suppliers he would usually use, but he did know about them and probably had contacts there. Did Ellie think there might be a market for that kind of toy in the town? Ellie was reluctant to comment, not wanting Billy to make any business decisions on her say so.

Then he told her about Harry coming home soon for Christmas and she suggested that Billy speak to him, and the rest of the family, about it first. All that Ellie did know, simply from observation, was that there were probably nearly as many middle- to older-aged people in the town as there were younger ones. These sets were much more expensive though, so it was not a decision to be made lightly. Was there any chance he could come by the same, or a very similar, set more cheaply (second hand but in good condition, for instance), to be used for demonstration purposes? Research into old train sets? There was nothing that Billy would love to do more in quiet times at the shop and at home.

That day, as Ellie put her coat back on and went to leave the shop, she looked up at the space immediately above the door, which housed a large, horizontal, rectangular-shaped window, in line with the top of the two window fronts on either side of the door.

"What did you say Harry does for a living, Billy?"

"He's a construction manager in the Middle East. Been out there for years now and loves it. Shows no sign of wanting to come home, though we all wish he would."

"Okay. So, I guess he makes things and is good with his hands, good at DIY, for instance?"

"Oh, yes, very practical. Does any work I need about the house for me when he's home, which isn't as often as I'd like. I'm really looking forward to seeing him."

"I'd love to meet him too, Billy. I'd like to ask him a few questions."

Billy beamed with pride. "I'm sure he'd love to meet you too, Ellie. I've mentioned you to him."

"Bye, Billy. See you soon."

"Bye, Ellie. Take care."

# 18

Maureen Enderby was also in a quandary about the Christmas window display but, unlike most of the other town shopkeepers, still had no ideas to show for it. The problem with being fiercely independent and somewhat aloof from other people meant that you didn't have many people to confide your doubts and insecurities to; she'd probably rather share them with a complete stranger than her closest friend, Bridget. She'd even tried, on occasion, to engage Frank in conversation on the matter, casually referring to the fact that she was struggling a bit, but no doubt everything would fall into place very soon. The first time, Frank had grunted agreement and said that, yes, no doubt she'd have a eureka moment very soon. After all, there was plenty of time. The second time, when there was no longer plenty of time, she'd injected a certain amount of unease in her voice, complaining at the same time about the stress the whole competition was causing her.

"Why not withdraw, if it's causing you that much

hassle? Haven't you got enough on your plate already, just running the shop?"

Maureen was aghast. "Withdraw? I couldn't possibly withdraw. It would be like admitting I have no… no… no… imagination or artistic flair, or whatever."

Frank's expression very much looked as though she might have hit the nail on the head, which caused Maureen to catch her breath. She had to put down the ornament she'd been dusting and sit down for a moment to recover.

"Do you think I don't have those things, and that's why I'm struggling ever so slightly?"

The penny dropped at last with Frank, as it usually did in the end, though it often took a while. He straightened up in his chair, very deliberately took off his glasses, put his newspaper down beside him, reached out and took Maureen's hand.

"Perhaps you need to look around you a bit more, love, for inspiration? You work so hard in that shop and here, you never seem to take a break, except when we're on holiday. When did you last just take the time to stop and look, whether in books or online or just down the street? I'm sure, no, I know, that if you just take the time, the ideas will come."

As usual, Frank was probably right. Maureen hoped so.

The next day, at lunchtime, she picked up her bag, put on her coat, and a sign up on the door, and went for a walk. It was a beautiful autumn day: the trees, gold, bronze and red, shedding as she walked; the leaves crunching under her shoes; the low sun glinting through the branches.

The slanted, protracted rays of the sun split the world in two: above, the vast expanse of blue sky, wispy clouds and unattainable treetops; below, the scented earth, pine cones and leaves. For the first time for a long time Maureen paused, looked around and took in a deep, deep breath.

She found a quiet spot by the palace and loch and took out her sandwich. The ducks and swans flapped and raced towards her expectantly. She scattered a few crust fragments towards them, smiling. They were noisily grateful but wanting more.

Suddenly and irritatingly, a conversation broke through the peace. It was a mother and child at the small swing park nearby, their voices carried by the still air that barely raised a wave on the loch. The child had previously been shrieking with delight as his mother pushed him on the swing, the creaking noise of which had now stopped.

"Come on, Joe, it's time to go now. We need to pick up Cat," Maureen heard as the mother obviously tried to heave her son out of the swing.

Struggling and kicking, he yelled, "Why? Don't want to go!"

"Ouch, Joe, that hurt. Please don't kick. We need to go and get Cat from school. She'll be waiting for us, like every day, you know that. I've told you before, she can't go home on her own, she's too young. Just like we'll come and collect you when you go to school, right? How would you feel if there was no one there to get you when you were waiting for us? Now, can I get you down and into the buggy, please?"

Joe appeared to be unsure that he was going to allow

that, preferring to stay in the swing. Jiggling his legs and pouting, he persisted, "Push, push, push!"

Sighing, frustrated and tired, the mother cast her eyes away from her son. She scanned the distance, through scattering leaves across the play park towards the high street, and had an inspirational thought.

Turning to Joe, with a slightly strained, excited expression on her face, she said, "After we've got Cat, we could go home and write a letter to Santa!"

"Why?"

"About what you want for Christmas."

"Why?"

"Because, if you write to Santa, he might get what you want for Christmas."

"A train, like in the toy shop?"

"I don't know, but you can ask."

Joe appeared to weigh up the proposition for a while. "Okay. Let's go and get Cat."

His mother caught him, laughing and kissing him, as he tried to extricate himself from the swing, and heaved him into the buggy, whipping him round her as she did so. They left, singing about the bus's wheels.

Maureen sat for a few moments thinking and absentmindedly feeding her lunch to the swans and ducks who now joyously and raucously surrounded her bench.

Very slowly, she smiled to herself.

# 19

Chrissy was loving life at the moment. The shop was doing well, she was kept busy and feeling fulfilled. She hadn't had time to see Debbie much but did make time to see Fran and Beth, who were more local. They'd had some raucous dinners at each other's places, taking the mickey, quite mercilessly, out of other people in town, Maureen Enderby and Councillor Blakeney amongst them.

Dad had visited and come with her to one of them. He seemed to enjoy the rowdy gossip and being teased and flirted with but afterwards quietly touched Chrissy's shoulder, on their way home, and said she should be careful, as she could be the butt of their jokes at any point, in fact might already be when they bantered with other people. She should get together with Debbie soon, who was a constant friend. Chrissy, slightly chastened, saw his point and called Debbie the following day.

"What are you doing on Sunday?"

"On Sunday? I've got a date!"

"A date? You mean a real date, with a guy?"

"Yes! I joined this dating site. It's amazing. Designed for less able-bodied people, whether physically or mentally. You should try it. It's all very safe and everything. We're only meeting for coffee at this stage. We've been messaging via the app though, and he sounds really nice. I've been wanting to tell you about it for ages but really wanted to do it face to face. I'll send you the website details. How about Monday, then I can tell you all about it?"

Chrissy felt guilty. Her friend had wanted to share something, and she hadn't been in listening mode.

"Monday would be fab. And be careful, okay? Call me when you get home after. Good luck."

"Thanks, and will do, Mum."

Chrissy felt quite anxious all day Sunday. Normally, this was a rest and admin day, after the work of the week before, but she felt restless. Beth texted her and asked if she'd like to come for coffee but Chrissy, unusually, declined, fibbing that she had a bit of a sore head. She wheeled about her flat, abstractedly doing housework and quite possibly overwatering plants. When her phone rang, mid-afternoon, and she saw "Debbie" flash up on the screen, she snatched it up, fearing the worst but not really knowing why. If anything had happened, it was her fault for not listening to her friend earlier.

"Debbie? Are you okay?"

Debbie laughed. "It's okay, Chrissy, I've had a fab time and I'm home now. He's a really nice guy. Looked just like his photo too, which, apparently, is unusual. He's a wheelchair user, like us, but very active. We talked about anything and everything. He's really easy to chat to and isn't just interested in himself. I really, really like him, Chris. Please look at the dating site too – you could do with a break from work. When did you last go out with a guy?"

Chrissy realised she couldn't remember. There'd only ever been one or two real "dates" in her life. Being in a wheelchair tended to kill romance: it put a whole new complexion on a guy sweeping you off your feet (wheels) and carrying you off into the sunset. Something in Debbie's voice stabbed at her insides though: jealousy.

She decided to ignore the question. "Just be careful, will you? There are so many weirdos out there. And there are particular weirdos who target women in wheelchairs, because we're even more defenceless than the rest."

"I know. Don't worry. The site is well aware of that and even more safety conscious. Everyone's rigorously vetted. I'll only meet him in a public place or with someone else for ages yet. In fact, you could join us and see what you think of him yourself? I've told him all about you."

For some reason the prospect of playing gooseberry to Debbie, and the fact that she'd already been a subject of conversation between her and her new man, caused a pain even more piercing than the earlier stab of envy. As soon as the call ended, Debbie saying goodbye in an irritatingly cheery and encouraging way, Chrissy pulled out her laptop and searched for the website name her friend had sent her.

Debbie was right: it did all look very legitimate and well designed. There were lots of pictures of wheelchair users of various age groups, including same-sex couples, holding hands and laughing either at the camera or each other; also a few with Down's syndrome. Other couples had less visible disabilities, the text below explaining that people with a history of mental health issues or phobias, or people who just didn't feel well or strong enough to look for romance in a more mainstream dating site, had successfully used "their more specialist and tailored service". The cost didn't appear too high either, particularly after Chrissy had searched on a few standard dating sites to compare. It was a bit more expensive, but the home page noted this was due to the additional security the company offered to its "more vulnerable" clients.

Looking at the joining process, Chrissy was impressed by the level of detail required, including references and a condition everyone was obliged to accept that their medical and other history must be provided to the company, for validation purposes and the safety of anyone they would come into contact with. This information was absolutely not shared with anyone outside the company and only used as part of the assessment process, the wording stated in bold type. The application form was reassuringly detailed, and Chrissy noticed a few questions that appeared to repeat themselves but with slightly different wording, in a way she'd seen before in surveys, intended to trip up dishonest people. More bold print below noted that the company used complex technological algorithms to assess everyone's application, which had had a near 100% success rate. Chrissy wondered how near to 100% and about the proportion that didn't quite get there but supposed that nothing was perfect.

A whole page was devoted to the "Dos and Don'ts of

Dating", including some pointers Debbie had mentioned on the call. Always meet in a public, and preferably busy, place; always tell someone where you'll be and roughly for how long; always have your phone with you and charged up; never meet until you've messaged a few times and feel comfortable to do so; get to know the person first; take someone else along, at least to start with, if you prefer, etc. Chrissy couldn't help but become excited at the prospect of meeting new people and moreover people who had the same, or very similar, challenges to the ones she faced. Not to feel an obstacle, a hindrance, at the very least an inconvenience, inferior, discounted, ignored, an embarrassment even; and the deliciousness of doing something slightly rebellious (she couldn't help smiling when she imagined what Dad would be thinking if he knew what she was doing) was almost intoxicating.

She found herself eagerly adding her personal information. She could attach the medical details tomorrow. She drafted, paused and thought, redrafted and, at last, happy with the content, clicked save. She would review and submit in the morning. Always better to sleep on an important decision, Dad said. Chrissy smiled to herself again. He would not, in his wildest imaginings, have considered this as one of those decisions, she was certain. Somehow, that made the prospect of actually submitting her application even more exciting.

# 20

Romance was also on Greg's mind, but in a more problematic, though (or therefore?) equally exciting, way. Even at this early stage of his relationship with Lola, he felt as though he was treading something of a tightrope. What on earth would it be like if things got more serious, which he intensely hoped they would? The last thing he wanted to do was offend or upset the Arsians, whom he really liked and which it would certainly not be in his best interests to do, in a small town such as the one they all lived and worked in. It wasn't small enough for everyone to know everyone else and their business, but it was common for everyone to have links with pretty much everyone else through mutual friends, acquaintances, colleagues, customers and fellow shopkeepers. He also had his business to consider, and mud tended to stick. If he put a foot wrong, he would be the subject of unfavourable gossip, which could result in lost custom, or at least make his life difficult and very unpleasant.

He was also acutely aware of Lola's brothers. He didn't

know much about them, and therefore they were probably bigger characters in his imagination than reality warranted. How protective were they of their sister? How strong was the Turkish culture in terms of accepting Western men as potential partners of family members? He knew they both had partners, and thought one was married, but had no idea whether their wives or girlfriends were Turkish or not, and he couldn't exactly ask Berk or Lola herself. He determined to ask a few discreet questions the next time Lola said anything about her brothers on the phone.

They'd called each other a few times since meeting at the bookshop event. To start with, they just exchanged casual, innocuous text messages, asking how they each were, how work or studying was going and what plans they had. Lola didn't always reply quickly, which initially sent Greg into a head spin, but she did always reply eventually. He forced himself not to respond immediately, resisting the desire to apply pressure and painfully aware that her studies had to take first place. He also had enough pride to avoid coming across as a needy and overeager potential boyfriend.

Then he'd taken the excuse of knowing that she'd had a particularly difficult assignment to complete, and it was the end of the deadline date for submitting it, to give her a call to find out how it had gone. She was obviously in the pub or students' union with her friends when she picked up. There was a lot of babbling and a bit of shrieking laughter and distorted music in the background, for which Lola immediately apologised.

"We're celebrating!"

"And is that celebrating because it went better than expected or just because it's over and you're drowning your sorrows?"

Lola laughed. Greg loved her laugh. It was deep, not giggly like a lot of girls. It sounded like it came from her chest, her heart, rather than just her throat.

"Probably a bit of both. How about you, how are you doing? Any reasons for you to celebrate?"

"Well, I've made a good start on the top-secret window display. It's coming along nicely. I should be able to put it up in a week or so. Actually, I do have a favour to ask. Once I've done it, could I send you a picture so you can tell me what you think? As an objective observer, I suppose, and to check I haven't done anything stupid. Would that be okay?"

"Of course, I'd love that! But, hang on, won't you have to kill me afterwards because I'll know the theme?"

"I thought of that. But then, I'd have to kill the whole town, wouldn't I, because everyone will know soon after then."

Lola laughed again.

"I suppose you would, 007, with a licence to sell bikes as well. That's really good news, though, as I know it must have caused you a lot of angst. I'd better go. I'll call you back in a few days when things are, well, less noisy."

And that's how it started. They called each other when something slightly out of the ordinary happened in their lives. Greg sent her a photo of his window display assembled, but not in situ yet, with the caption underneath: "I thought I'd have a dress rehearsal first and take M's, Q's or L's, that's Lola's, advice before releasing to the public. The downside is I might, as a licenced secret agent, be ordered by Councillor Blakeney to kill you now. Before that happens, could you please, please let me know what you think?"

Lola was seriously impressed but, after consideration and a bit of research, suggested a few changes.

"Thanks so much, Lola. You've been great about this, especially as you have so much going on. I really appreciate it."

"I enjoyed doing it. It's been a great distraction, just like the book Dad gave me. How are you doing with yours?"

So, then they messaged when they reached critical events in the books they were reading, using deliberately vague language to avoid plot spoilers, hoping they would swap books afterwards. It became a bit of a competition in cryptic language substitution and word circumnavigation.

Greg confided some of this to Ellie but nothing to his parents. He hadn't told them about any of his casual girlfriends, probably because he never intended them to be anything but just that, and they were never likely to meet, nor would he want them to. This was different in every way, but the significance of sharing Lola with them was terrifying and the prospect of back-pedalling if it didn't work out with her made him feel physically sick. He just couldn't do it, at least not until after they'd seen each other again and Greg knew more about her feelings for him (if any, he kept telling himself). He did talk to Ellie a bit, given that she knew the Arsians and had probably sensed something of the situation. She was sensitive enough not to use that as an excuse to pry but listened sympathetically to anything he had to say and offered gentle encouragement.

Then Greg had an unexpected breakthrough. Lola called him one evening to say that her brother, Kaan, would be bringing his new girlfriend at Christmas, whom she'd never met as she'd been at uni when they'd visited Lola's parents before. Berk and Defne were ridiculously excited, she told him, and would no doubt turn the day into a totally overblown celebration, which might well scare the poor girl off. It gave Greg the permission he needed to ask about both brothers and their partners, wife in the case of the older one, Lola confirmed. She didn't know much about Kaan's girlfriend, but Yusuf's wife was a bubbly blonde from Liverpool, who was a perfect match for her serious brother and adored by all the family. Did Lola and her family celebrate Christmas, or were they strict Muslims (he'd done a bit of research)? Not strict, was the answer, and in any case, Turks had a celebration similar to Christmas but later on, in fact in the New Year. It included a Christmas tree, Santa, the lot. But Lola's family sort of did both, as they had so many non-Muslim friends and Defne, in particular, loved any excuse for parties and family get-togethers. A bit hypocritical and greedy, she confessed, but why not make the most of both cultures?

Greg agreed, enthusiastically. His heart lifted and he felt as though his Christmas had come already.

# 21

Activity and excitement levels were high in the council offices too. Sylvia had had the brainwave of inviting a journalist from the local paper into the building for meetings with Councillor Blakeney and the other judges, all of which she'd set up and hosted herself, with a great show to all attendees of how she herself was absolutely critical to the success of the project.

The prospect of his own interview had made the councillor distinctly nervous and uncomfortable, even though he was fairly used to dealing with the press, no doubt because he knew Sylvia had primed the journalist with the kind of questions to ask but failed to share this information with him. As it happened, the meeting went off pretty well, he thought, and he even succeeded in getting a photo of himself, solo, alongside the published article, a coup that put Sylvia into a black mood for the rest of the week. She retaliated by absenting herself frequently from the building under the pretext of visiting each of the shopkeepers in the competition to check on their progress, leaving him high and dry to answer calls and get his own tea and coffee, minus biscuits as she'd been too busy to stock up, she said.

Sylvia did faithfully visit every competitor in the course of the week and then booked time with Councillor Blakeney to discuss her findings. Things were progressing well, she said, and everyone was on schedule to complete their window displays by the deadline. She'd need to go out a bit more often, once the work started to take shape, and she'd arrange the afternoon for judging before the end of the following week. This would be tricky, she emphasised, as there were five judges in total and she only had access to diaries for the two on the town council. She hoped the councillor would agree that she was working very hard to ensure that the whole thing ran smoothly, so it reflected well on council members and all the work the council did. She paused at that point, to allow the councillor actually to get a word in, as long as it was the one she wanted to hear. Stunned into submission by her verbal onslaught, Councillor Blakeney concurred, and Sylvia ended the meeting.

*This really is getting out of hand*, Jim thought, mopping his forehead with a handkerchief after she left the room. He desperately wondered if he should have a word with Councillor Rao about an exchange of assistants. How was it that he and Joyce got on so well when he, Jim, had not the slightest idea how to manage Sylvia? Ajay would surely make a better job of it than him, and Joyce seemed a much more reasonable and, well, less volatile, person. For a few seconds, Councillor Blakeney dared wonder whether

Sylvia's behaviour was anything to do with her "time of life", as his wife, Moira, would put it. He tended not to talk about work in any detail with Moira, conscious that much of what went on in the office was confidential. Not that he didn't trust her to be discreet, but it was just so easy to let things slip out in conversation, without even meaning to. Yes, that's what he'd do, speak to Moira in the first instance. She could sometimes be quite insightful about people's behaviour, certainly much more so than him, at any rate.

Meanwhile, Sylvia was having a, not very quiet, moan to Joyce in the kitchen area.

"Honestly, Joyce, if it weren't for this competition, I'd have jacked this job in by now. Jim's job is so boring, normally, so that means everything I do is boring too. I mean, who's interested in street cleaning and waste management, for goodness' sake? Even the planning applications aren't as fun as they used to be. You can tell now who's going to get the go-ahead and who won't as soon as they land on your desk."

"I am, actually, and my niece Clara's doing a project about it at school. Waste management and recycling, that is, not the others."

"But what you and Councillor Rao do is so much more interesting. Visiting schools, talking to teachers and pupils, going to libraries. Now, that I would enjoy."

"It's not all as interesting as it sounds. The teachers and pupils, not to mention parents, can be a nightmare. To be honest, I'm almost as fed up as you. Feel as though I'm stuck in a bit of a rut and need a change. Perhaps we should do a swap?" Joyce giggled. "Councillor Rao's nice enough, but he's a real stickler for timing and has OCD about stationery. You should see his face when you walk into his office with a brand-new notebook in your hand. The other week he actually had the cheek to ask me whether I'd definitely used both sides of the paper in my old one and showed me how I should flip it over to do that! Can you believe it?"

Sylvia laughed, but she wasn't convinced, feeling that she could manage a bit of OCD much more easily, and to much greater reward, than she could Jim Blakeney.

The women returned to their desks, Joyce with a mug in each hand, one of which she took into Councillor Rao, Sylvia with just one, which she carefully put down on the desk beside her keyboard. She pulled up her contacts list for the e-mail addresses and telephone numbers of the external competition judges and copied them across, with names, to a blank document, leaving a large space to the right for notes regarding availability. By the end of the afternoon Sylvia had calculated roughly how long the judging of all the shop windows would take, made several calls, consulted councillors' calendars, filled all the spaces on her document and reviewed the council room booking system to check availability of the conference room at those times. No real problem there: it was coming into a relatively quiet time, just before Christmas.

Then Sylvia checked her own office and personal calendars: she'd certainly be present at – no, an essential part of – the judging, Jim Blakeney or no Jim Blakeney, and then they would all convene back at the council building to discuss what they'd seen and cast their votes.

That reminded her: she clicked to another page on her screen and added "Create ballot paper" to the ever-open competition to-do list. Finally, she drafted an e-mail to all judges with the shortlist of dates and times, quickly reviewed what she'd typed and clicked send.

Sylvia sat back and let out a very deep sigh. She'd been so engrossed, she'd forgotten all about her tea, which was now cold. Never mind, it would soon be time to go home. With a bit of luck, she'd have responses from everyone by the end of the week, then she could organise some catering for the judging meeting. She was determined to make a bit of an occasion of it. In fact, she could put Christmas decorations up in the room, maybe even a small tree, just to keep everyone in the mood after seeing the window displays. That would be a nice touch, and she'd get some favourable comments from the judges, which she'd love Councillor Blakeney to hear. Then there'd be the arrangements for the award ceremony soon after, of course, probably in the same conference room. That would be an even bigger occasion, with all the shopkeepers. She'd need to work out a good date for it and book the room and catering. She quickly created a task and reminder for the next day.

Yes, Sylvia was very pleased she'd thought of the idea of the shop window display competition. A stroke of genius on her part, in fact.

# 22

The shop windows were, indeed, at various stages of transformation, although some had really only been partly cleared to enable the process to start. The shop holders discovered that timing was everything: they couldn't do anything too early, leaving them either starkly exposed to the competition or with the windows in a prolonged state of disarray just before Christmas, possibly impacting sales; nor could they leave the work too long, risking a last-minute, unforeseen disaster. Many mulled over this quandary for some time and some enlisted help so they could delay action. Maureen considered asking Bridget and decided against it. The successful outcome of Frank's offered advice produced an uncharacteristically humble wife who needed a man's strong arm – and DIY tools – to put the plan, he'd been partly responsible for germinating, into action.

So, they spent evenings and Sundays together at home and at the back of the shop, constructing Maureen's idea, of which Frank enthusiastically approved when she returned from her walk and, hesitatingly, voiced it to him. He climbed up into the loft at home and the rafters of their garage to bring down, not without difficulty, all sorts of items that Maureen had been long nagging him to get rid of, with a smug smile on his red and sweaty face. Maureen raided the grandchildren's toy boxes and dressing-up box for materials and brought out her mother's old sewing machine, which Frank serviced and she restocked. The machine hummed of an evening while Frank watched TV downstairs, and Maureen caught herself humming along with it: snippets she remembered her mother singing while she sewed and Maureen sat on the floor at her feet, sorting her tin of cotton reels by colour.

Beth rediscovered their property's basement, saying there wasn't enough room in the flat or shop to work in. Her response to Chrissy's cheeky comment at the shopkeepers' meeting in the council offices sparked the idea. One morning, she opened the cellar door, flicked the light switch and peered downstairs. Of course, she and Fran had looked down there briefly when they viewed the property before buying it, but had been so intent on opening the shop and making the flat habitable that they'd ignored the potential of the space downstairs. It didn't even feel damp, and, as far as she could see, the floor and walls were sound, with no gaps to allow for infestation. There were a few items of rubbish but, once cleared and cleaned, the walls whitewashed, more light, table and heater added, seats and shelving installed, it would be perfect for her purposes.

Ellie was helping Billy, and Harry would be home in

time for the final installation. She'd shared her idea with him, and he was beyond excited. They'd also shared many a conspiratorial cup of tea at the back of the shop, drawn diagrams to plan out their ideas and Ellie had, to the startled surprise of passers-by, clambered into the window spaces yet again to take measurements, Maureen watching intently from across the street.

Berk and Defne worked together on his creation at home. Lola had been excited when they'd told her about the plan on the phone.

"That's a brilliant idea, Dad, well done! And yes, of course you can do whatever you like with it. I'd love to see it when it's done. Please send a photo as soon as it's ready."

Berk thought about asking her how Greg's creation was going but decided against it. Defne had no such reservations.

Lola laughed, admitting that she'd seen the more-or-less-finished article.

"It looks like I'm in quite a position of power here. I might just have to blackmail both of you! I could do with a bit more money just before Christmas."

Sylvia visited them all to review progress. She needed to be sure, of course, on behalf of Council Blakeney, that everything was going according to plan. She had now arranged the judging and would shortly be e-mailing them about the awards ceremony (ignoring the councillor's plea for her not to call it that, as it made it sound like the Oscars and would inflate people's expectations), to which everyone would be invited. Her report back to Councillor Blakeney took half an hour of his precious time and left him with his head in his hands after she closed the door behind her.

Chrissy enlisted her dad and Debbie, although the former could only help at weekends and the latter had much of her free time absorbed by her new man. Chrissy was forgiving of this as she had now fully signed up to the dating website herself, although she'd shared that only with her friend because, she told herself, she didn't know what would come of it and wanted to avoid the pressure of the inevitable, and possibly unnecessary, anxious paternal questions. She would wait and see and then share with him when there was anything worth sharing.

She'd found a few guys who looked interesting, one of them more than the others. He was about her age, an electrician by trade, still living with his parents as he was saving up for a deposit on a flat, and a keen gardener, which appealed in particular. There was a photo of him, sunburnt and blond hair windswept, standing in a garden, leaning on a fork, grinning at the camera, an elderly, frail-looking woman next to him, her hand on his other arm, smiling up at him. Chrissy was quite entranced by it. Part of his "About Me" referred to voluntary work he did in old people's gardens when they couldn't manage by themselves; usually the clients he did electrical work for. *How many young men of that age would do that?* she thought to herself.

The text also referred to his dad, who was currently in hospital but likely to become a wheelchair user for the rest of his life. The guy himself (there were no names: the site prided itself on the complete anonymity it guaranteed until people were ready to share that kind of personal information) was obviously not a wheelchair user, but he'd had mental health issues, which left him feeling he didn't want to use a standard dating agency. He worked too hard, and sometimes unsociable hours if he was doing shifts or on call, so had limited time to meet women. He'd turned his life around, so he said, by keeping active, working hard and helping others. He had no preconceptions of whom he might meet; he was completely open to trying a relationship with anyone.

Chrissy wondered. She couldn't quite fathom why someone as fit, active and good-looking as him would want to be involved with someone like her, Debbie or anyone else who signed up to this particular dating service. It didn't make sense. But then, as everyone so often said these days, disabilities are often not visible. *Don't judge people by appearances.* Perhaps, in her wheelchair-bound state, she was turning into one of those people who did just that. Wheelchair user or not: she wasn't using any other differentiation for the appearance of health and ability, which made Chrissy very cross with herself indeed.

*What have I got to lose? I can always backtrack.*

She clicked connect.

# 23

Greg was thoroughly ashamed of himself to discover that he was desperate to see Lola again. He'd vigorously and frequently told himself that he would not interfere with her studies in any way. He didn't even know if she had a boyfriend already; she hadn't said, and he hadn't asked, for fear of getting an answer he didn't want to hear. He told himself it wouldn't matter if she did, as he would just patiently bide his time and carry on seeing her as much as possible, so he would eventually win her over in place of the boyfriend.

But today he felt far from patient. Perhaps it was his triumphant conviction that he'd got rid of Gizza once and for all, and in a way that salvaged his own conscience, or maybe it was that he'd spent the previous day at his parents' and let slip a few things about Lola that he hadn't intended to impart at all but that just spilled out in the joy and relaxation of the moment. Of course, once Greg shared that there was a girl he really liked whom he'd seen a few times and who seemed to like him, their obvious and openly expressed delight only made him want to please them even more. When it came to the "when do you think you'll see her again, son?" from Dad, and his response that he really didn't know as she was away at uni and too busy with her studies to be home very often, it had felt like a knife blade to the gut. He really didn't know, and he hated not knowing. He could be patient, as long as he knew when it would be.

So, the next day, uncharacteristically, he'd posted a sign on the shop door, apologising to his loyal customers and saying that a personal emergency (well, it was, wasn't it?) prevented him from opening that day, donned his cycle helmet and sped off to the railway station. He'd calculated that he could be at the uni by mid-morning, as he'd been up so early in a state of restless anticipation, and therefore back by late afternoon, after which he could spend the evening on cycle repairs due to be completed later in the week. While feeling guilty about the stock of work staring back at him from his laptop screen, he persuaded himself he wouldn't lose any custom at all as people would just come back later, and he was prepared to bust a gut to catch up afterwards. He just hoped the gut busting would be worth it.

He'd also researched the uni campus layout and pinpointed the medical sciences building. As he approached it, he knew it immediately, not only from the map but also Lola's laughing description: "It looks more like a prison than a uni building. Sometimes it feels like it too!" Of dreary grey brick and several storeys high, it even had bars at some of the uppermost windows. *To prevent the students from throwing themselves out when they get bad grades?* wondered Greg. It certainly looked formidable and unwelcoming.

He'd also researched where the bike stands were and easily found one with space. After carefully attaching and locking his bike, he headed, hesitatingly, towards the main door. Would he even be allowed in? Security was probably really tight in places like this these days, with the risk of terrorist attacks or attempted arson by dissatisfied students or academics driven mad by working in such an ugly place…

Luck was on his side. A gang of anxious and noisy students, obviously in a hurry to get to an exam room in time, was being ushered through a couple of open barriers by the security guard, just waving their ID badges. Greg quickly extracted his book, which he'd been reading on the train, from his rucksack, opened it and pretended to study it intently, mumbling under his breath as though memorising the text, while he flashed his public library card at the guard and followed the group through. He realised afterwards that he was not only sweating profusely but also pumped with a giddy feeling of excitement and almost invincibility.

The next challenge was finding Lola. He knew from what she'd told him that she was in the building for lectures, seminars and lab work every day of the week that she wasn't in the hospital, but he had no idea of the balance between the two. However, he also knew that her student accommodation was some distance away, so guessed she would hang out at the building, main library or cafe in the breaks on the days she was there. He checked his watch: 9.45, so the next session, whatever it might be, would be at 10.00, according to what Lola had told him about her timetable. But where, in this cavernous vault of a building, would she be if, indeed, she were in it at all?

Then Greg suddenly remembered Lola saying she hated Tuesday mornings because she had a lengthy lecture on anatomy with a particularly boring professor. Dr Goodall, Goodwell, what on earth was it? If only he'd listened more closely. Why hadn't he contacted Lola to tell her he was coming? No, that had never been an option as she might have said no, and he really needed to see her today. Soon. Now.

"Excuse me, I've an appointment with a professor, but I can't remember his last name. Goodall, Goodwell? Can you please help me?"

The student looked, bleary-eyed and confused, at Greg for a moment, and then slowly grinned.

"Poor you. Good-For-Nothing's in lecture room twelve at the moment. I'm just heading that way for his next bout of torture. I can show you the way."

Greg mumbled his thanks and followed him to the lifts, hemmed in with buzzing, fidgety or glassy-eyed students, and then along endless corridors with painfully graphic anatomical pictures and tatty notices on the walls and a constant traffic of young people, armed with files, books and laptops, intent on looking anywhere but where they were going.

The corridor was empty, however, when they reached the door of the lecture room.

"I'll leave you here and go and grab a coffee before the next class, if that's okay? Oh, and good luck with Good-For-Nothing."

"No problem at all. Thanks very much for your help."

Greg sank down on a bench outside the door. What on earth was he doing? Lola had no idea that he was there. She wouldn't be looking for him and would just exit the room and pass by in a stampede of students. He'd be completely invisible, and she'd have no idea he'd even been there. Some consolation in that, at any rate. He wouldn't be embarrassed if she never even knew. But he so wanted to see her, to talk to her, if at all possible, to touch her.

The next ten minutes passed painfully slowly. Greg had almost resolved on escape when the lecture room door was flung open and students filed, largely noiselessly, past him. Obviously, Dr Goodall/Goodwell had induced a state of near coma in most as they processed like automatons, chins almost on chests. Lola was at the end, accompanied by a female (*thank God*, thought Greg) fellow student. She looked beautiful, as ever, in her student attire of jeans, hoodie and trainers, but tired and anxious. Her brows were still knitted from the obviously intense and very complex lecture the students had all just been subjected to. She stopped, confusedly, as soon as she saw him, and her eyes lit up – first with astonishment, then what Greg hoped was almost undisguised delight, followed quickly by an intense anxiety – when they met Greg's.

"Greg! What are you doing here? Is everything okay?"

Greg realised, and internally kicked himself for it, that

she must be fearing something awful had happened to bring him there so unexpectedly.

Lola's friend diplomatically whispered into Lola's ear, taking her arm for a moment, smiled at Greg and disappeared down the corridor.

"No, nothing. Sorry for worrying you. I just, well, I just really wanted to see you."

"That's nice. I'm glad to see you too." It sounded genuine, not just polite, to Greg.

"Are you free for a coffee or something, or are you busy? No problem if you are, but if you have any space today, maybe we could fit it in somewhere?"

Lola smiled, slowly. "I've actually got the most massive of headaches coming on and am going to go back to the flat to get some aspirin and study from there. Do you want to come with me?"

Greg was ecstatic but quickly tried to hide it. "I'm sorry to hear it. It would be great to go with you."

Later, Greg didn't remember much about what happened immediately afterwards, except Lola's "it'll be fine, you can pick it up later. Or in the morning" when he told her about his bike. They sat on the bus, thighs comfortably rubbing, holding hands but only looking at each other occasionally because there would be ample time for that soon. Lola's half-shy, half-teasing smile made Greg's whole body tingle with anticipation. The worried look had disappeared, replaced by a happy and relieved acceptance. Passengers stared at them, some disapprovingly but most congratulatory. A black bitch Labrador, passing with a passenger, licked Greg's hand. Lola leant over Greg to pet her and the smell of her hair and perfume made Greg feel grateful that he was sitting down, otherwise his knees might have buckled underneath him. It felt to him as though everyone on the bus, everyone in the world, must know how they were feeling and what they planned to do as soon as they got to Lola's place. *Please God, let it be possible,* thought Greg.

The flat was empty, as Lola had known it would be. They walked up the stairs, step by step, hand in hand. Lola unlocked the door and pulled Greg through. After checking that they were, indeed, alone, she dropped her bag with books, papers and laptop onto the carpet of the untidy lounge and led him through to her bedroom. She faced him, for the first time properly, with her back against the door, shook off her coat and almost ran at him, pushing him onto the bed.

# 24

Sylvia's arrangements had gone well, and everything was now in place for the remainder of the competition. So much so that she felt a lull in the proceedings, which wasn't conducive to a good mood as it afforded fewer opportunities for her to torment Councillor Blakeney. All she could do was escape from the office as frequently as possible on the pretext of checking the shop holders' progress, although even this could only be stretched so far.

Eventually, even Joyce took her aside in the kitchen area and mentioned she'd overheard Councillors Rao and Blakeney talking about her absences. Joyce hadn't been able to catch what had been said but she was certain she'd heard Sylvia's name mentioned and not in a favourable, though distinctly serious, tone. They were obviously conscious of being overheard and had spoken very quietly, heads locked together, over Councillor Rao's desk. When Joyce told Sylvia the following week that the occurrence had been repeated in Councillor Blakeney's office, Sylvia suffered serious alarm.

She visited and spoke to Gwyn about it one Friday evening over a glass of wine.

"Do you think they're trying to get rid of me? And after all the ideas and work I've put into this wretched competition. How dare they?"

Gwyn considered for a minute or two.

"Would it be such a bad thing if you didn't work there anymore? You've been itching for a change for ages, and all you do is complain about the place and most of the people there. Maybe it's time to look round for something else? I know it's not a great time of year for it, but people leave jobs all the time. You should at least start the process, and it might even make you feel a bit better. You should update your CV too. I can help you with that if you like."

Sylvia knew her sister was right, and the prospect of taking control of the situation, rather than waiting for something probably dreadful to happen, was appealing. And the work she'd done on the competition to date would stand her in good stead and give her something interesting to add to her CV, even if she didn't see it through to completion, although it was unlikely this would be the case so late in the year and with her notice period to be served. She could already hear in her head the words she'd use to describe what she'd achieved and the skills required. "Good communication, attention to detail, dealing with members of the community as well as internal colleagues, organisation second to none, excellent problem-solving, time management and diary maintenance skills…" It would be an impressive list. Sylvia brightened up immediately.

"You're absolutely right. And even if it takes a while it'll be worth it. I'll be a model employee in the meantime too, just to make sure I don't give them any more grounds for complaint. I'll need a good reference after all."

So, Sylvia phoned a few friends and mentioned, in strictest confidentiality, that she was looking for a new position, asking them to keep an eye out for her. This they eagerly agreed to do, playing down Sylvia's pessimistic assessment of the current state of the employment market, which buoyed her up further.

She also started buying and perusing the Jobs Vacant section of the local, weekly newspaper. There were still a number there, although the majority of roles was online. Sylvia subscribed to a few job websites too, although the amount of information there, much of it not relevant, was daunting. Sylvia had only had one job prior to her current one, for a few years after leaving college, so it had been a long time since she'd done anything like this. She'd just assumed she would stay at the council until retirement, as most other people there did. It was a good job that she'd previously really enjoyed and was still envied for by friends and family. That was before Jim Blakeney came on the scene, of course.

One evening, after a particularly trying day at the office, throwing her handbag, coat and scarf down onto the sofa of her flat's small but cosy living room, and collapsing next to them so she could ease off her shoes, she heard a ping from the bag. It was an alert from one of the recruitment websites. A new vacancy had been posted that met her criteria: administrator at a local council office, reporting to a councillor responsible for town planning and waste management, including recycling. Very responsible position, requiring much experience, strong administerial skills and, ideally, knowledge of planning and recycling procedures. Other prerequisites were communication, time management and people skills. Sylvia stared, wide-eyed and disbelieving, at her phone screen: this sounded like her very own job being advertised!

Sylvia snatched for breath, but the air caught in her throat and made her choke. Her face burnt and eyes streamed from the effort of rebutting the attack of confusion and fear. She gasped repeatedly until, at last, she managed to slow her breathing down and hold her chest to try and quiet her painfully thumping heartbeat

After a few minutes, with an effort, she dropped her phone on the sofa next to her, heaved herself up and went to the kitchen, hand reaching desperately for the door handle and shaking as she twisted on the tap, to pour a glass of water, which she downed in large gulps. Still holding her chest and concentrating so hard on breathing slowly that the rasping hurt, she went to the fridge and poured herself a glass of wine in the same glass. Checking the measure, with straining, blurred eyesight, she topped it up, staggered back into the living room, spilling some, and collapsed on the sofa again.

Calmer and clearer thinking returned eventually. It just couldn't be, Sylvia reasoned. She could easily be mistaken. The role was being advertised by an agency and there was no mention of which particular role was being offered at which particular council. There were several it could apply to. She was being paranoid, after her recent conversations with Joyce. For added reassurance, she picked up her phone again and called Gwyn, hands still shaking

Thank goodness her sister was in her favourites, otherwise Sylvia thought she'd have had to wait a while before her fingers were steady enough to touch the right numbers. As expected, Gwyn was calm and matter of fact, to the point that Sylvia detected a note of exasperation in her voice, but then her sister was in the middle of cooking dinner and she could hear shouts and bangs from her niece and nephew in the background as they, apparently, fought while laying the table.

At last, just to get rid of her, Sylvia suspected, Gwyn sighed, resignedly.

"Well, I guess there's only one way you're going to find out for sure."

"And what's that?"

"Contact them and say you're interested in the job but it depends which council it's at. If it's yours, you could give yourself away. It might be worth the risk, though, if you're actually interested in the role. You are looking at roles like that, aren't you?"

"Well, yes, I suppose I have been, though I did want something a bit more different to what I'm doing now. It *would* be with different people though and is a really good match as far as experience goes. I'm confident they'd at least have to interview me."

"Well then, that's decided. Apply and see what happens. I must go now, Syl, the potatoes are just about done, and the kids are driving me mad. Give me a call in the next few days and let me know how it's going. Bye."

A few hours later, Sylvia clicked submit on her online application.

## 25

Ellie had been seeing Billy frequently over the last few weeks, not only because of their combined effort on the shop window display, which was progressing well, but also because he'd invited her home a few times and she'd reciprocated. They felt easy and comfortable in each other's company and talked about anything and everything. Billy reminded Ellie a bit of her own father, long dead now, and Billy asked Ellie's advice on family matters, in particular concerning Susan after Andy finally, fingers crossed, passed his exams and went to college.

Billy and Susan had had a trying time when Andy was a young teenager, *not surprisingly without his dad there*, thought Billy; *teenage boys can be difficult at the best of times, as I remember from Harry. Though he wasn't at home long enough in his teens to show too many black moods to us!* It was during this period of Andy truculence that Billy had been at his angriest with Harry, though he'd scrupulously hidden and never mentioned it to anyone, for fear his son would find out and stay away even longer or travel further afield. That was when Andy could really have done with his uncle as a father figure, he felt. *Not a great role model when Harry had upped and left, discarding both parents as soon as he possibly could*, Billy mused, as bitterly as it was possible for the mild-mannered old man to feel. They certainly wouldn't want Andy copying that behaviour when he was older.

Harry had been good with Andy when he was home, though, Billy had to give him that, always taking time out to spend with him and bringing him back a present Susan couldn't possibly have afforded. And he'd offered to support his sister and nephew financially, Billy knew, though Susan had forbidden him ever to mention to Harry that she'd told him. She'd thanked her brother and declined, saying he was very kind and generous and she knew where she could come if she were ever desperate, but her independence was important to her. Harry knew better than to push it with his proud and stubborn sister so had simply set up his own bank account for them, depositing payments monthly and larger, one-off amounts when he got his bonuses at completion of a project or gifts from particularly grateful clients.

Billy was determined to host a family celebration too, to welcome Harry home, and wanted both Ellie's presence there and her advice, along with Susan's, on how to go about it. They talked about all the options and costs; Susan offered to help with providing food for the buffet; Ellie eagerly joined her, and the two women started up a friendship themselves, based on mutual care for Billy, the toy shop and town, interest in and excitement about the competition and their shared fate as single parents of one son. It was an odd combination of personalities: Ellie, with her almost childlike vivacity and mix of openness and shyness; Susan with her reticence, combined with stoic determination. There was mutual respect for the things they collectively held dear, and Billy was happy to see it.

Inevitably, Billy and Susan talked a lot about Harry, and Ellie found their chat deeply interesting because of the work he did and where. It was in places that sounded exotic and which she would never have dreamt of visiting. She looked forward to meeting him at the welcome home party, though Billy forbade anyone from calling it that.

One morning at the toy shop, while Billy and Ellie were drinking tea at the back, Billy mentioned Chrissy Dickson and Ellie realised, with shame, that she hadn't seen her properly since the event at the council office to launch the competition. She'd seen her from a distance along the high street and waved, yes, and also through the shop window while passing and Chrissy was busy with customers, but not properly, no.

"I'll go along and see if she's got time for a chat when we're done here."

As Ellie approached the florist shop, she heard voices coming from the open space behind it. It was a beautiful day, mild for the time of year, almost windless, and with a pale blue sky, across which perfect white clouds gently glided in procession. Ellie peered through the shop window and saw it was empty. Rather than needlessly disturb Chrissy's break, apparently outside, by calling her through with the noise of the shop bell, Ellie walked on past the door, to the far end of the shopfront, and looked round the corner. Chrissy's shop was one of the few on the high street at the end of a row. There was a gap between it and the next building, not wide enough for a car but certainly for a small cart, Ellie surmised, probably loaded with coal, in days gone by. Curiosity getting the better of her, she entered the gap. It was grassy but not too overgrown. On the right was a high fence, which marked the border of Chrissy's shop's premises, and Ellie could hear voices floating over it: Chrissy's, laughing, she recognised; the other one, male, more serious and interspersed with the sound of grunting and mallet hitting wood, was unknown to her. On the left was the wall of the building next to the shop, which extended further behind. She carried on walking. The pathway came to an abrupt end at another fence blocking the way in front of her, but there was a gate in it. It was old, the wood dark, decayed and splintered, but it looked serviceable, and Ellie noticed new hinges and a new padlock and chain on the side of the handle.

Ellie was seized with a curiosity to know what was on the other side. A biggish rock lay just in front, and to the right of, the gate. It looked damp, mossy and slippery, but Ellie had her trainers on so the grip should be safe. She put her left foot on gingerly, grasping the top of the gate with her left hand. It felt okay, so she heaved herself up. Being small, she was only just able to see over the gate to the overgrown path that began at the bottom of Chrissy's premises and ran along parallel to the street behind all the shops and residences for as far as she could see. She could dimly make out fences and walls marking the end of the buildings' boundaries, some with gates, but the weeds in the pathway, given free rein, were dense and as high as the tops of most of the fences. Except for the space behind Chrissy's, that was. That had been cleared, and she could see another gate in the middle of her fence, also padlocked.

Ellie got down slowly and walked back round to the front of the shop. She looked through the window again. It was still empty. Slightly reluctantly, but with no idea why, she opened the door and heard the tinkle of the bell above her. The sound of the voices outside immediately ceased. Peering through to the back of the shop, Ellie saw that the door, accessing the outside space behind, was open. In a few seconds she heard Chrissy's wheelchair rumbling up and down on the ramps each side of it and then her smiling face was there, below her.

"Ellie! How lovely to see you! How are you? Have you come to shop, or is this just a social visit?"

Ellie smiled. "Purely social, I'm afraid. But only if you've the time. You look busy outside. I can come back another time."

"No, not at all! We're making the most of the good weather, before winter really hits, to do some work outside. You should come and see."

Mentally noting the "we" (maybe with her dad?), Ellie agreed and followed Chrissy outside.

A young man, tall, muscular, dressed in long shorts and a T-shirt, long blond hair plastered to his forehead with the effort, was hammering a post into the freshly dug earth at the end of the "garden", which was currently a mass of tilled, composted (Ellie could smell) earth with a path of paving slabs laid down the middle.

"We're planning to put in polytunnels and grow our own flowers and vegetables or at least give it a go."

Chrissy's voice and face exuded excitement, pride and, well, happiness, Ellie could see. She turned again to look at the young man who appeared to have effected this transformation.

"Oh, sorry." Chrissy was mortified. "So rude of me. Ellie, this is my new friend, Gary."

# 26

These days, Chrissy had to keep pinching herself to ensure she wasn't dreaming. Work on the window display was progressing better than she could have imagined. On top of that there was Gary. She occasionally snatched her breath away in panic when she remembered she almost didn't sign up to the dating site at all. Just a few days later, she'd been contacted to say that someone had responded positively to her interest in him – Gary. He was asking if she'd like it if they messaged each other directly via the app as he was keen to chat with her. Chrissy thought about that first message she would send for hours.

It had to be casual, but not too casual; serious, but not too serious. Her hands shook as she eventually typed on her phone, petrified she'd send it part way through by mistake, just because her fingers were all over the place.

*Hi. It's Chrissy. Thanks very much for contacting me. I'd very much like* (she'd written "love" at first and then deleted it in panic) *to chat with you directly too. Can you tell me a bit more about yourself? I'm a florist, as you probably saw, which I absolutely love* (no problem to use that word when it was about her livelihood, surely?). *I really hope you enjoy your work too.*

After sending it, Chrissy was consumed with mortification. What an idiot she sounded, when she read it back to herself. Smug, self-satisfied, too serious, to the point of being boring? In the end, she threw her phone away from her in disgust, determining not to waste a single moment more on the whole stupid thing. Until it pinged back at her in a matter of minutes.

*Hi, Chrissy. Great to hear from you. Gary here. I'm an electrician by trade and I love my work too as I get to meet lots of people, some of whom are pretty amazing. I also do gardening work, which is one of the reasons I liked your profile. I don't get much time for socialising, so it can be pretty lonely when I'm not working. That's why I signed up to the site. I wonder if you feel the same?*

And that's how it all started.

They began messaging regularly: in the morning, to say what the day had in store, and in the evening about how it had gone. Then one day, tired and with aching fingers, hands and wrists after a particularly tricky round of table centrepieces, Chrissy messaged to ask if it would be okay for her to call him instead and then sat back, holding her breath. She jumped in her chair when the phone instantly started ringing.

"Hi, it's Gary. Are you okay, Chrissy? Has something happened?"

His note of anxious concern caught at her heart, then she immediately panicked that she could easily have frightened him off.

"No, no, I'm so sorry, Gary, I didn't mean to worry you at all. If you were worried that is." She'd have kicked herself, if she could, at her own assumption, in case it was wrong. "It's just that my hands ache after a hard day in the shop, making these really fiddly table decorations."

Chrissy couldn't stop a giggle at the memory of the woman in her crocheted hat, knee-length knitted poncho, hand-dyed, rainbow-coloured tights and suede ankle boots, with large, colourful stitching, who'd come into the shop a couple of weeks back to request the pieces for another member of the Handcraft Guild, for whom they were holding a farewell party, and then returned to collect them that day. One of the things about being a wheelchair user was that you got a really good view of people's footwear. She heard Gary laugh too and returned to the present.

"Sorry, I was thinking of the customer who ordered them. She was, well, let's just say, unusually dressed."

"Well, at least you're laughing about it now," he said. "Was it a difficult customer? I've had my share of those too, but mainly they're just great."

And they'd exchanged stories of tough and good customers, funny incidents along the way, mistakes made, wasted goods and effort, and big rewards in the shape of grateful clients with sneaked presents added to generous payments. Eventually, realising the time and how long they'd been talking, Chrissy ended the conversation with the suggestion that they call, instead of message, every evening. Gary immediately agreed.

Then one evening, Chrissy let slip about the mess that

was behind her shop. When she'd taken the place on it had been quite a tidy, lawned garden with a narrow, bare border round the edge but, given her circumstances, she hadn't been able to maintain it and, with the shop itself being higher priority and money tight, hadn't thought to employ anyone to do it for her. Gary immediately offered to come and take a look at it to see if he could do anything to help. If she was comfortable with that? Maybe her friend – Debbie, was it? – could be there too? He'd like to meet her at some point anyway.

Chrissy's breath was taken away at the prospect. She hadn't even considered meeting him yet – it was too early, surely? Certainly, struggling to bring to mind the site's recommendations, she felt it was. But what harm could there be, particularly with someone else there? And, all being well, she'd probably have met him in a few weeks anyway. Why delay? And the garden, if you could still call it that, was in dire need of work, and the weather would soon turn bad, and it would be impossible then. Within seconds, she'd convinced herself it would all be fine, as long as Debbie could be there, of course.

"That would be great, but are you sure? I know how busy you are."

"Well, it could only be out of working hours, and you'll have to check with Debbie too. Just let me know when she can come, and I'll see what I can do."

Feeling sure that Debbie wouldn't approve of her moving forward with Gary so quickly, Chrissy, at the same time reluctantly and excitedly, called her. Debbie was disapproving but also sympathetic and happy for her.

"Well, if you make it in a couple of weeks' time, and just carry on calling and messaging in the meantime, I guess you won't be too far ahead of the guidelines. Of course I'll come. I'd like to meet him too. And make sure you tell someone. Your dad, maybe? Have you told him about Gary?"

Of course Chrissy hadn't, but it appeared she'd have to now. No, wait a minute, she'd tell Billy. He wouldn't say anything to her dad if she asked him not to. She would tell her dad eventually, of course; it just felt premature until she had a better idea of how things were going to go with Gary. Billy was much closer anyway, just in case they did need someone to come to their aid. *Like damsels in distress*, Chrissy thought rather grimly. One of the biggest downsides of being in a wheelchair was that you really did feel quite helpless sometimes.

So, when Chrissy messaged the next morning she could give Gary a couple of dates that worked for both Debbie and Billy, and when they spoke later that evening, he told her which one suited him best.

"That's it settled. I'll see you then."

He'd been even more good-looking in the flesh than his online photos. He still had his work clothes on under his coat as he'd come straight from a job, he said, but he looked good in the dark-blue company overalls with the firm's name and logo on the back and his first name on the front. They contrasted well with his long blond hair, tied back at the nape of his neck for safety reasons, he laughed. Chrissy could see Debbie's admiring look, immediately suppressed so she could return his handshake. Chrissy herself was suddenly overcome with shyness, but Gary behaved in a very businesslike manner, suggesting immediately that he take a look at the back, before it got too dark. He'd also like to take photos, if that was okay with Chrissy, as that's what he usually did with his gardening work; it helped with the planning and time estimate. Chrissy just nodded, somewhat dumbly, but came to her senses once outside and showing Gary the space.

The grass was completely overgrown and the borders now invisible under a mass of weeds. The only work that had been done out there since Chrissy had the shop was for her dad to put ramps up to and down from the back step for access, at the same time as he'd done so at the front door. The area had become a bit of a dumping ground too for wood and other rubbish taken from the shop during the refit. That would all have to be cleared first, Gary said. Chrissy should also have a think about what she wanted to do with the space. Would she like more border, for instance, so she could grow stuff, or did she just want it as low maintenance as possible? She could even consider paving at least some of it, so she could sit outside, or install a shed for storage space if she needed it. Did she have gardening equipment, as he could bring his own, if not? That would probably be better anyway, as he was used to his own tools and worked better and more quickly with them. Chrissy confessed she didn't and hadn't even considered any of this but would have a good think. Debbie said she would help her.

After he'd taken photos, they all went back inside and Chrissy made tea, which Gary drank quickly and immediately got up to leave, reaching for his coat and saying he was desperate for his dinner and sure they were too. He'd message and speak to Chrissy the next day and it was really good to have met Debbie too. He was endearingly formal in his handshaking again, laughingly telling them not to worry, he wouldn't do that every time he met them but felt it was important on the first occasion, and waving from his company van as he passed the shop, having picked it up from round the corner. Debbie was very complimentary in her chat afterwards and Chrissy could feel her own cheeks burning. Debbie had to remind her to call Billy to let him know everything was fine.

That had been about a month ago. Since then, Gary had come round at least once a week to work at the back and do any odd jobs in the shop that he spotted were required. After the fourth time, Chrissy decided she didn't need Debbie or Billy anymore, though she did call Debbie after Gary had left a couple of times afterwards. Then she simply forgot. Bar one time, when he'd met Ellie too, he only came out of shop hours and always parked his van away from the high street, even if this meant lugging heavy gardening tools that bit farther. He was a bit precious about the van, he said, being completely reliant on it to do his job and with it not being his own, and it could easily get damaged on the busy road.

The space behind the shop was cleared of rubbish quickly and then Gary could hack at the grass, weeds and baked earth while Chrissy painted the fence, brought refreshments or simply watched, approvingly. To help remove stuff from the garden, and in anticipation of bringing new things in, Gary said, one of the first things he did was improve access to the back via the alleyway next to the shop, clearing the fence-high weeds and installing new hinges and locks on both gates. What seemed like very quickly, Gary was saying they needed to go to the garden centre to get the plants and other things she wanted.

That was one of the best afternoons of Chrissy's life. They arranged to meet there, which was a shame, but Gary said he was coming straight from a job again. He lifted her chair from the car in the car park, although she didn't need him to, and looked after her quite proprietorially as they moved together slowly between the tables of plants, bushes and tiny trees, picking up whatever she gestured towards so she could have a closer look. They debated, jokingly, the relative merits of the herbs, admired the colours of flowers and foliage and discussed the appropriateness, or otherwise, of plants for different spots of Chrissy's garden, as that's what she could start calling it now, Gary said. She particularly loved the curious, speculative or smiling looks from the other customers and would have given almost anything to know what was going on in their heads.

Job done and car loaded, without even discussing it they made their way to the cafe, where Gary insisted on buying them both coffee and cake, which he brought to the table for her.

Chrissy just didn't want the afternoon to end so, when they'd finished, she said she wanted another coffee and Gary said, "Good idea." He got up again, returned, and they discussed for the second time where each of her purchases was going to go, Gary grabbing his own, unused, paper napkin to draw a diagram of the garden, complete with initials marking the spot for each plant. Then he spoke about the polytunnels he'd helped his older clients erect, some quite small, and how useful and satisfying they'd been in allowing them to grow their own vegetables. Chrissy's eyes lit up at the idea, and they were soon heading back to the garden centre to buy the pieces for it and more compost. Gary pointed out that the beauty of it for Chrissy was that they only needed a low one, as she wouldn't be able to reach high anyway, and this would keep the cost right down. She did have plenty of room for a long one though, to get the maximum benefit. Chrissy hung on his every word. He also insisted on driving back with her to the shop before returning home so he could help her unload and take her purchases, which were considerable by now, round the side of the building and into the garden via the gates. Usually fiercely and stubbornly proud of her independence, Chrissy found it deliciously relaxing to accept his help, eagerly and gratefully.

There were a couple of things about Gary that jangled in Chrissy's mind when she dwelt on them, so she usually emphatically dismissed them. He was reluctant to talk about his past and his family. His father's health was not good, she knew that much, and he'd been in trouble as a teenager, but that's as far as he'd ever go, and Chrissy didn't feel she could probe further. Didn't want to, in fact, for fear of pushing him away. Maybe, given time, he'd open up to her more. After all, there was a lot she hadn't shared with him either. Like the fact that she was, hesitatingly, petrifyingly, incredulously but wondrously falling in love with him, for example.

# 27

Things were hotting up at the council office, and among the shop holders, about the window display competition in more ways than one. The day of judging was now only a few weeks away, and the judges would visit all shop windows not once but twice that day: once when it was light, so they could fully appreciate the sight, and once when it was dark, to get the benefit of any illuminations the competitors had used.

Sylvia had phoned all the judges again, or their assistants, to double-check everything was in order. She had also received a favourable response from her job application. They would be delighted to offer her an interview and asked her to propose some dates. Sylvia did so and received a reply thanking her and saying they would be in touch again soon to confirm the date and time of the interview and the location. This should be in the next few days. They then thanked her for her patience.

Patience, what patience? Sylvia was itching to know. A couple of times, while Councillor Blakeney was out of the office, on the pretext of retrieving something from his desk, she had a good nosey round his room, searching for documents that might refer to the job advert. All of the filing cabinets were stacked by Sylvia's own desk, and she had keys for them herself, so he wouldn't have put anything in those. The only places he would have put something he didn't want her to see were the drawers of his desk or the few cabinets against the wall next to the window. She tried the desk drawers. The bottom, deeper, one was locked. The top one was unlocked and contained, right at the back, so she had to put her hand all the way in and scratch it about, crablike, to find it, a small bunch of keys. Hands shaking, and constantly looking up at the door in case anyone came in to find her, she tried the keys in the lock of the bottom drawer. It took a long time to insert each of them both ways up, but none fitted, as far as she could tell. That left only the cabinets against the wall.

Sylvia breathed deeply. This was going to take longer than she had expected.

The sudden ringing of the phone split the air and made Sylvia jump and gasp. She really didn't want to answer it in there as it could be Councillor Blakeney himself phoning her (she could hear her own desk phone ringing outside as well) and he might realise she was in his office. As calmly and quickly as she could manage, she returned the keys to where she'd found them in the top drawer, thankfully remembered to pick something up from his desk, planted a rather shaky, casual smile on her face and walked out of the door, heart thumping in her chest.

She could see that desperate measures were going to be required.

Lunchtime saw Sylvia striding down the high street to the florist's. She'd enjoyed her chats with Chrissy about the competition, but now she had her own business to transact. She knew Chrissy would be discrete. Don't they say that about florists, a bit like priests and doctors, client confidentiality and all that? After all, it could be a bit of a betrayal if a florist let slip that a customer's husband had bought an expensive bouquet of flowers when said customer had not been the recipient.

Chrissy beamed when the bell rang and she saw Sylvia entering the shop. Sylvia was somewhat taken aback by the change she noticed in the young woman since the last time they'd met. Chrissy's smile was assured, and her face was alive, no, glowing, with confidence and a bright prettiness. She was a very pretty girl, Sylvia had noted that before (such a shame she was in a wheelchair, she could have been a stunner with the right hairdo and make-up), but this was different; she was enhanced somehow, more real, more present, more alive.

"Hi, Sylvia. Lovely to see you again. Are you here about the competition?"

"Hi, Chrissy. You look well! No, it's me just shopping, actually. I've, well, I've had trouble sleeping lately. It's lonely when I go home at night and I'm allergic to pretty much all animals, so I can't get a pet. I just wondered if a few plants could make a difference… Caring for them is supposed to be therapeutic, isn't it?"

The concern on Chrissy's face made Sylvia feel slightly nauseous with guilt.

"Yes, it is! And they like being talked to, especially

by women, it's been proven! What are you looking for? Some colour or just green, and how much time do you have for maintenance? Some are very low maintenance, it's all about the watering. People tend to over-, rather than under-, water them. Will you need pots as well?"

Half an hour later Sylvia was struggling slightly back up the road with three heavy bags containing four plants and all their accoutrements, half of which she did fully intend to take home with her. The rest she carefully extracted from the bags on her return to the office and carried into Councillor Blakeney's office, knowing he was out for the whole day. She arranged the two plants carefully, in their new pots and saucers, on top of the cabinets along the wall so that they were immediately above the keyholes of the drawers, humming quietly to herself.

*Chrissy's right, this is therapeutic!* she thought to herself and wondered why she hadn't had this most brilliant of ideas earlier in her career.

To Sylvia's surprise and carefully concealed delight, Councillor Blakeney announced to her later that day that he'd be taking a couple of days off at short notice. His mother, who was in a care home farther north, had had a bad turn and he wanted to visit her. Sylvia did her best to look and sound concerned and sympathetic and was successful enough to be rewarded by an unexpectedly grateful and slightly chokey response from the councillor.

The next day she was in his office first thing, armed with watering can and spray. After raising the window blinds, she turned to look behind her at the plants and saw the iridescent light of the low sun reflect off their shining, searching, deep green leaves. They really looked as though she had woken them up from a deep, fulfilling and blissful sleep and were now reaching for the light, like human beings stretching off stiff limbs and opening dazed eyes to the morning.

Sylvia sighed deeply with satisfaction then pulled herself together and quickly and silently retrieved the keys from the office desk, as before.

She tried them first in the cabinet nearest the window, careful to water and spray the plant, tidy the soil and rather noisily rearrange the pot while she was doing so. Her hands shook a little, but she was surprisingly calm. All keys, both ways up, no luck.

She caught her breath as the first key turned in the lock of the second cabinet, first time. There were three drawers. It would take too long, and look too suspicious, for her to open and search them all right now. She would have to be patient. Sylvia noted the number on the key, returned the bunch to the desk drawer, watered and rearranged the second plant and left Councillor Blakeney's office.

When she returned to her desk, Sylvia saw she'd received a notification from the recruitment site. The date and time and location of her interview were confirmed: the very same council building she was currently sitting in, and the interviewer was Councillor James Blakeney.

# 28

Billy was so keen to get the whole family back together as soon as Harry arrived home that he arranged the "party" for the day after his flight, despite Susan's protests that poor Harry would be jet-lagged, tired and in no fit state to face the lot of them less than twenty-four hours after sitting on a plane for nearly ten hours, even though he was flying business class.

Somewhat chastened (he had to agree that she had a point), Billy promised Susan he'd talk to Harry first, to check he'd be up for it and, if not, he'd push it back a day or two.

Harry laughed when Billy broached the subject during their last, short call before he left Oman.

"Does Susan think I'm getting old, that I can't bounce back quickly any more after a long flight? I'm flying business class, remember, Dad? I'll catch up on e-mails, do some reading for work and then I'll be ready for a sleep for most of the rest of the flight to London. Don't worry, I'll be fine. Whether you lot will be fit to see me is another question altogether."

Billy was delighted, particularly that Susan had been proved wrong. She was so much like her mother sometimes, argumentative just for the sake of it.

Harry had insisted that no one was to collect him from the airport. The company paid for a taxi, didn't they, so why should anyone in the family spend the time or money? Billy could hardly contain himself while waiting for his son to arrive at the shop, where he was coming straight from the airport. Harry had insisted on that too, not wanting Billy to close it, even for an hour, to await his arrival at home. He was dying to see the place after so long, anyway, he said. Billy was itching to show it to him after all the changes he and Ellie had made and talk about what they wanted him to do for the window display, of course. He'd touched on it with Harry in messages and even e-mailed him a diagram drafted by Ellie, complete with measurements. Harry had been impressed.

Billy almost ran out of the shop when he saw the taxi drive slowly past, looking for a space to pull over. He waited, almost hopping on the spot, while Harry got out with his rucksack, dropped it on the pavement, leant over to speak to the driver through the open front passenger window, handed him some notes and raised a hand in farewell. He was beaming when he turned to face his father.

"I've persuaded him to take my suitcase home and leave it in the shed at the back. It'll be safe there, won't it? Then I can just walk back. The fresh air will do me good. Hello, Dad. You haven't changed much; in fact, you look younger now than the last time I saw you."

The men embraced, tears in Billy's eyes. Harry picked up his rucksack and they went into the shop.

"Ellie! It's Harry, he's here at last!"

Ellie came through from the back, smiling a little nervously, to find a tanned, good-looking man in his mid-fifties, with very short but still thick, sun-bleached hair, clean-shaven apart from a little stubble, also bleached, and with Billy's grey-green, kind eyes. Harry saw a petite, pretty woman, possibly a little younger than himself, with clear, blue-grey eyes, shiny long, silver hair tied at the back and wearing skintight leggings that revealed slim, well-toned legs. *A runner or a cyclist*, thought Harry. *Interesting*.

Billy introduced them, proudly on both sides, then went through to the back to put the kettle on. Harry immediately asked Ellie about the window display, and she showed him the space while he got out his phone and scrutinised the diagram Billy had sent him. He also thanked her profusely for helping his dad with the shop.

"I'm really pleased and grateful, as it's his life now, and every bit of help means he can carry on, and more easily. He's been struggling a bit in the last year or so, to be honest. Thinks he's as well and fit as he's always been, but age is finally catching up. It's one of the reasons I came home this time. And I'll be able to help him more in the future. I haven't told anyone in the family yet, as it's only just been finalised and I wanted to say it in person, but I'll be coming home permanently in about six months' time. I'm going to tell them all tomorrow, and I plan to look for somewhere to live while I'm here. Maybe you could help me with that as you must know the area a lot better than me. It's been so long since I was here for any length of time."

Ellie was flattered to be admitted into his confidence and at the suggestion that she could be of any help.

"I'd be glad to but I'm afraid I don't know much about the market as I have no intention of ever moving from my house. Susan would probably be of more help. She'll have more contacts too, through the school and work."

Billy called them through for tea and produced an extra special tin of biscuits he'd bought specifically to celebrate Harry's return. He was now even more excited about the family get-together and told Harry all about it. After chatting non-stop for about ten minutes, he was happy to sit back and watch Harry and Ellie enthusiastically plan for installing the window display, starting the next morning.

He was even more pleased to see them chatting enthusiastically at the family event the following evening, which was, of course, over-catered, despite Andy's best efforts to sweep clean the buffet table. Harry was telling Ellie all about Oman and his work there. Susan noticed it too and she and her dad winked at each other, like a pair of naughty school children. It was almost as good to hear as Harry's news that he'd be coming home for good in about six months' time and his intention to look for somewhere to buy while he was here, which he stood up to announce rather formally. Billy couldn't stop himself clapping his hands, and everyone joined in. There were hugs all round again, to which even Andy reluctantly and sulkily submitted, and Billy insisted on popping out to buy bottles of fizz to celebrate properly.

"About time you grew up and settled down," was Susan's rueful comment to her older brother as she gave him a peck on the cheek.

# 29

Quite a crowd gathered for the evening's judging. Not only were more people free from work but the slow, relentless drizzle of the morning had given way to a pale, watery sunshine that radiated surprising warmth. That had faded in the gloaming, but there was still no real chill in the air as the townsfolk stood, talking in low tones, outside the main door of the council office building.

Sylvia was at the forefront of the judges, of course, and led the way through the small crowd, motioning the direction of travel. Councillor Blakeney had decided, for reasons of scrupulous fair play, to be absent from the process. The townsfolk followed the group at a respectful distance, still whispering and speculating as they walked.

They visited the shops in a random order that had nothing to do with proximity, the shop holders' names having been pulled from a bag for both tours. Maureen and Frank were waiting outside hers, ready to greet Sylvia and the judges, and shook hands with each of them in turn again. A stiff formality enveloped the scene, apart from a few nervous giggles from the crowd, instantly hushed.

An awed silence descended while Frank entered the shop to turn on the window lights. There were a few muffled gasps as the scene unfolded before them, people craning necks to see round the judges in front, those at the back prodding the coats of the more fortunate ones to ask them to describe the view.

It was a traditional nativity scene, modernised and reimagined by using dolls, dressed as Mary, Joseph, four shepherds, one of which was a child, three kings and the baby Jesus. Jesus was, literally, a baby doll, the largest of the lot and lying, covered by a miniature, homemade blanket, in a doll's cradle centre stage, so the effect was somewhat incongruous at the same time as being utterly charming. Mary and Joseph were about twenty centimetres high. She was dressed in a pale blue skirt suit, white blouse and high-heeled plastic shoes, so looked a bit like an old-fashioned air stewardess; Joseph was in army khaki with a red beret and boots. They were both sitting in an appropriately, for them, sized plastic car with no doors or top. Mary was driving and waving to the audience at the same time. It almost looked as though they were just setting off on holiday.

The shepherds were smaller and obviously part of a farm set at one time. They were standing outside a shelter, made from plywood, filled with straw and containing a number of woolly sheep, made for the purpose. One of the shepherds had a pitchfork in his hand and another a shepherd's crook. The young shepherd was sitting down with a lamb in his lap and also waving at the gathered spectators. In contrast, the kings were solemn and majestic. They were made from varicoloured material, were obviously stuffed and wore even brighter costumes. All had cardboard crowns, one gold, one silver and one black, covered with tiny "gems". They wore flowing robes and cloaks, and pantaloon-like trousers protruded below the dress of one of them; they all wore ridiculously large and misshapen material shoes that they would not have been able to take a step in, but they completed the picture of the exotic. Of course they had gifts too, at their feet: the obligatory box, presumably containing gold, a jar for frankincense and a goblet for myrrh.

Almost more eye-catching than the characters themselves were the items surrounding them. Maureen had lain out her best seasonal goods from the shop: Christmas decorations, candles, ornaments, toiletries, jewellery, sweets and biscuits, so that the overall impression was one of cheerful, bright and colourful excess. The whole scene was lit up by a network of tiny lights suspended above, with a rich dark blue sheet of light material above them, to resemble a clear night sky. A small placard lying immediately in front of the doll's cradle had "What will you give this Christmas? Let us help you find it here!" written on it in bold, gold type.

The judges nodded approvingly, to Maureen's obvious delight and Frank's sighing relief as he put his hand on her arm, whether to steady her or himself, it was impossible to tell. The judges scribbled hurried notes on sheets of paper. One of them took photos. Sylvia waited patiently while they talked quietly amongst themselves and then ushered them along the road.

They went to Chrissy's next, who saw them coming and came outside into the darkening gloom. She'd been deeply disappointed that Gary, apologetic as he had been, was unable to join her because of a job (*in the evening in the winter? she thought. It can't be electric work, and he can't be gardening in the dark, surely?*). However, she saw Billy, Ellie and someone who must be Harry, from what Billy had told her, preceding the group comprising Sylvia, judges and curious townsfolk, which had swelled slightly since leaving Maureen's. *Like they've headed them off at the pass to save me*, thought Chrissy, nervously, but she was deeply grateful. It was at times like this that she really missed her dad. Billy quickly took her hand and whispered an introduction to Harry, who smiled and shook her hand. Ellie bent down to give her a reassuring kiss on the cheek while she took her hand and whispered, "It'll be fine. You've done an amazing job."

That she had. After the judges arrived and they exchanged greetings, Chrissy clicked on her phone. Gary had set it all up for her. As if by magic, the pale lights in the window display came on, revealing a frame, around the window space, of abundant sprigs of holly, ivy and mistletoe, some woven together, some just touching, but a continuous loop nonetheless. White fairy lights blinked intermittently (Gary had set that up too), enhancing the deep, rich green of the leaves and the red berries and sharp spikes of the holly. Within the surround was a coverage of sprigs of dried flowers of all shapes, sizes and colours, held together with dainty, thin, shiny, silver ribbon. Bowls of potpourri completed the picture. Chrissy had deliberately left the shop door open, so the scent of the foliage and potpourri emanated out onto the street, and the crowd breathed it in deeply, murmuring their appreciation.

But the focal point was the fountain. Gary had found it for her in an antique place he visited to source garden ornaments for his clients. It was a perfect size, about that of a large serving dish, standing up on a pedestal about twenty centimetres high. Its old stonework was mottled with age and the elements, chipped in places, smooth or green in others. The mechanism worked perfectly, again thanks to Gary. Water cascaded slowly from the top, lit up by the tiny silver speckles they'd added to it. A Christmas wreath surrounded the base, one of Chrissy's classics, with orange, red and green leaves, white, green and red berries, pine stalks and cones, beech nut husks, teasel, cinnamon sticks and dried thistle and heather, all arranged in a perfect circle.

More notes and photos. The judges and crowd were becoming quite animated now. The wind had also picked up and clouds scuttered across the slither of moon, which reflected in the puddles on the pavements. It felt like rain, or worse, was coming.

# 30

Berk and Defne were starting to get anxious about the weather changing, while they waited outside the darkened shop, when they saw the crowd approaching from down the road, Sylvia at its head.

Defne, who was holding Berk's hand tightly, turned to him and gave her dazzling smile, all pearl-white teeth, brightened in contrast with her almost mahogany-coloured skin, large gold hooped earrings swinging and shining in the street lights.

"It'll be fine, darling. The display is amazing."

Berk wished he could feel as confident, but he smiled back and bent to kiss his wife's cheek.

Formal greetings with Sylvia and the judges over, Berk went inside the shop and turned on the lights in the front window.

The effect was startling, as the single figure in the window, and all his accoutrements, almost filled the entire space.

The king – he was wearing a very impressive crown, made from some type of metal, which reflected back the dazzle of the lights directly above – was about half human height and standing erect, proud, chest out, chin up, eyes staring. His clothing was sumptuous (Defne had even sacrificed one of her oldest kaftans), comprising many layers of gorgeous, colourful, in some cases gold-embroidered, cloth, cut away at the front to reveal each level and bound round the waist by a wide, gold, satin belt, tied in a knot. Gold tassels fell from the ends of the knot towards the floor. Just resting on his shoulders, so only the edges were visible, was a velvet cloak of deep crimson, attached at the neck by a wide, gold chain. Only the gold toes of his slippers were visible.

His hands were partly concealed by wide sleeves, but fabulous, jewelled rings adorned every finger. These were only visible because he was holding a beautiful, dark wood casket with gold hinges and clasp.

Even more stunning than his clothes were his shining, jet-black locks of wavy hair. Rather incongruously, given the abundance of clothes below, he was completely bareheaded apart from the crown, though there was a reason for this, which soon became evident. His hair cascaded down, also shining in the light, past his broad shoulders, and met with his huge, equally lush beard at the top of his chest. His skin was the colour of walnut, beautifully lined round his dark, heavily lashed eyes and above his equally dark and finely trimmed eyebrows.

Around his feet were spread all kinds of barber's equipment: scissors, razers, brushes, combs, products in beautiful, decorative bottles. And in front of it all, similarly to Maureen's display, there was a gold placard, with beautiful, elaborate script on it:

"I wanted to look my best to visit Him, so I went to Berk's Barber Shop first."

There was a low rumble of laughter as the crowd appreciated the joke. It had turned chillier now, the wind had picked up and carried with it drops of drizzle, so people were obviously starting to feel cold, even with their thick coats on, and were trying to button them up more closely at the neck or stamping their feet to restore circulation. They were impatient to move on and even started to walk along the road while the judges finished taking notes and photos and briefly conferred.

Greg's bike shop was next on the agenda. Ellie had made her way there straight from Chrissy's. Lola had also managed to get time away from university and was waiting outside with Greg, holding his hand until Ellie approached, but not dropping it quickly enough for it to escape her notice. She smiled broadly at them both and put her finger to her lips, motioning that their secret was safe with her. They both smiled back nervously.

The crowd and judges caught up. Greg also used his phone to turn on the shop's inside lights and there was a sharp intake of breath from the crowd as the scene unfolded before their eyes.

It was the classic flying bike scene from the film, ET, but it filled the entire window and was painted almost alarmingly brightly, the flaming orange of the sky contrasting starkly with the iridescent white of the full moon, the dark shadow of Elliott and his bike, carrying a covered ET in the basket at the front, three silhouetted riders following them, and the mountain and treetops behind. It had been painted boldly, with clear lines showing the figures, their bodies and bikes in full movement, the branches, leaves and even pine needles of the trees. The picture resembled a photograph in its radiating, and at the same time frozen, representation of action, intense drama and emotion.

The floor of the window space, rather like Berk's, was covered with bike accessories, including everything included in the scene above: baskets, bells, lights, seats, pedals, wheels, tyres, inner tubes and mending kits. They were interspersed with Christmas tinsel, sparkles and pine cones, as though they'd dropped from the trees in the portrait above.

The proceedings progressed more quickly now. The appreciation of the crowd was muffled as it struggled with the increasing chill, but the response was a favourable one, even Greg could see. He and Lola smiled at each other secretly and she took his hand again as soon as people started to move on to the next location.

It was Fran and Beth's turn. Also waiting just outside their shop, they appeared confident, a little smug even, as the crowd arrived. They waited until everyone had gathered in front of the shop window, and then a few seconds more for pure dramatic effect. Inside, it was obvious the lights were on, however what looked like a heavy red curtain had been hung on the inside of the window so that nothing was visible. They both disappeared inside the shop to slowly separate the curtain and bring the scene to view.

It was truly enchanting. A miniature "train" of small matchstick boxes, covered or painted as books, filled the whole window space, skirting actual books, all with Christmas themes, from the classic *A Christmas Carol* to the children's book *The Night Before Christmas*, and everything in between. The "books" were presented in minute detail to resemble the actual books, some of which accompanied them in the window. The whole scene had been decorated with tinsel, glitter and shiny stars, and interspersing the cardboard and real books were bookmarks of all descriptions, standing upright like trees along a railway line. A colourful placard at the front of the window read:

"Where will your next book train take you? Come in, and we'll help you find out!"

There were appreciative murmurs among the onlookers and Fran and Beth beamed at everyone and each other in turn.

The judges were now standing slightly apart from the rest of the group, quietly conferring, some of them gesticulating. The crowd hushed and strained to listen, while it tried hard not to look as though it was doing so, to what they said. Sylvia waited patiently for a few minutes and then gestured to move on, once the customary photos had been taken. Only one more to go.

Billy couldn't recall the last time he'd felt so anxious. *Probably at the time of the Arab Spring when Harry was in the Middle East and I was transfixed by the awful scenes on TV*, he thought. Ellie had walked there straight from Greg's to join Billy and Harry. Ellie stood next to Billy outside the shop, Harry on the other side, and gently wound her hand round his. Billy turned and gave her a weak smile. Harry put his arm round his father's shoulders.

Sylvia and the judges approached first, followed by the group of spectators, obviously relieved that they would soon be able to return to the warm and dry. Harry and Billy waited for almost everyone to be assembled before both entering the shop to turn on the window lights and start the display.

The lights were subdued. Most illumination came from the several, star-shaped fairy lights draped at the back of the window space in front of a black cloth, like a night sky. Another train, this time a toy one comprising engine and four carriages, was moving across the raised, white floor, as though it were covered with snow: around miniature buildings and fenced fields of farm animals, past trees and metallic plates, representing frozen lakes, through towns and stations with platforms and waiting passengers, up and over small hills, and then…

Then it climbed, zigzagging on a railed structure immediately in front of the window. Up and up, left to right and right to left, people gasping as they expected it to fall or fail, but up it still went, slowing and straining a little but strong. Then it disappeared into the darkness at the top, until Harry, who hadn't exited the shop, flicked another switch and the light from the second window came on, showing the train traversing the space at the top of the door and descending in zigzag fashion again on the other side, where an even more joyful scene unfolded.

Here, crowds of model people lined the rails. Miniature bunting hung from buildings and tiny flags had been attached to some figures' hands. Full-sized flags were stuck into the floor of the window space. It was as though the train had achieved an incredible feat that everyone had come to witness. It rattled slowly down the incline at the window, everyone again watching its progress with bated breath, anticipating disaster, wound round the floor and rolled into the station, where it came to a halt.

The response from the crowd was spontaneous. There was a round of applause, muffled by gloved hands. Billy grinned and hugged Harry when he came out of the shop. Ellie was hopping on the spot, whether out of excitement or to keep warm, it wasn't clear. Harry hugged her too, apologising by saying he thought she looked cold.

The judges conferred for a few seconds and then Sylvia suggested they go back to the council offices where there were refreshments and they could continue their discussions in the warm. The crowd dispersed, slowly, chatting as they left.

Sylvia determinedly led the judges back up the road. She'd withdrawn her application for her own job, requesting her personal details not to be shared with the employer. She got the distinct impression they'd guessed why but didn't care. She'd set up a meeting with Jim Blakeney for the following week, when he was back from another trip to see his mother. She'd have it out with him then.

# 31

The following day the judges were due to confer again, the consensus from the previous evening having been that they wanted to sleep on it before casting their final votes. Their decision would be announced the day after that, later than planned, but the quality of the displays had been unexpectedly high and very competitive, they apologised.

The high street was buzzing with talk of the judging and what people thought of the window displays. Some discussion became quite heated as locals plumped for one or other of their favourite shops or shop keepers. Crowds gathered again in front of the windows. Billy, amongst others, was proud and pleased to experience a small surge in sales as people came into the shop to get a closer look at how the train travelled across the doorway. They asked a lot of questions, which Ellie and Harry were there to field, and many said they hadn't thought of a train set for a Christmas present before but would certainly add it to their list of possibilities now. Billy basked in the glow of attention as he and his son stood behind his, for once, full and untidy counter, a noisy queue forming on the other side. Ellie scurried back and forth to and from the space behind the shop, furnishing them both, and herself, with much needed refreshments.

Chrissy had a busy day too, of people ordering Christmas wreaths. She'd decided on a promotion, following the window display competition, and was offering 20% off if people paid up front during the week after the judging, 30% if they bought more than one. She was grateful for the distraction. She hadn't seen Gary for almost a week, allegedly due to his busy period in the run-up to Christmas. ("You wouldn't believe how people go to town with all these gaudy Christmas lights, want advice on the set-up and then hassle you when things go wrong because they haven't followed it to the letter and managed to overload the whole system, especially in older properties with dodgy wiring.")

Admittedly, he'd been lavish in his apologies and meticulous in responding to any messages she sent, but they'd fallen out of the habit of speaking regularly on the phone and that familiar little voice inside Chrissy, which she tried hard, but could never quite manage, to dismiss, kept saying, "I told you it was all too good to be true."

She felt worse as she'd planned to tell her dad about Gary when she called him the night after the judging to tell him how it had gone. When it came to it, she chatted breezily enough with him to impress even herself, which made her feel worse, but decided on the spot that she'd leave telling him until after she'd actually seen Gary again. Another clump of earth added to the heap of anxiety.

She was glad also, after she'd shut shop, cleared up and looked satisfyingly at the day's takings, to have the further distraction of going to Greg's shop to pick up some deliveries that had been left at the back after he'd rushed off early to join a meal with Lola and her family. He'd very quietly and nervously told Chrissy, when he came to bring the keys and alarm fob, that they were going to tell Berk and Defne that evening that he and Lola were "an item". Chrissy smiled, sincerely pleased for them, despite the unavoidable pang of jealousy, and reassured him that she was sure it would all be fine.

"They're lovely, broad-minded people, aren't they? And from what I've heard, will probably be very pleased that she has a healthy distraction from her studies, which she'll finish soon anyway. Remember what we were told Berk said at the meeting at the council offices?"

Greg looked obviously, even painfully, relieved.

"Thanks, Chrissy. My head says the same, but you can't help feeling nervous, can you?"

It was pitch black by the time Chrissy eventually left the shop. It had been a day much like the evening before: grey, blustery, the leaves spinning in mini tornadoes on the pavements, the clouds threatening rain at any moment. Chrissy knew she'd have no problem getting into Greg's shop. He'd had a wider door installed not long after he took it on, following a sudden and large influx of triker clients. He'd also put up ramps more recently to encourage parents with pushchairs (and, Chrissy suspected, visitors like her, as she'd been in there once or twice since the council meeting).

She unlocked the door, flicked on the light switches, turned off the alarm, re-locked the door behind her, leaving the key in the lock so she didn't put it down somewhere and lose it, and rolled through to the back, just about manoeuvring between leant-up bikes on the walls, on their way to being repaired. She unlocked the back door, leant forward to pick up the items that were sitting on the back step, reversed and returned to put them on the counter, as Greg had requested. As she passed back through the repair area, she thought she smelt something oily but assumed this was coming from the many bottles on a shelf on the wall, obviously used to lubricate and mend the bikes. She continued to wheel towards the front door. It was only then she heard a strange, low humming sound coming from somewhere at the back, followed by a crackle. She stopped, wondering what it was and where it was coming from, and then, seconds later, an exploding flash of blinding light propelled her out of her chair and sideways across the room into some new bikes on stands at the side. She lost consciousness almost immediately.

Maureen Enderby was so surprised and alarmed by the explosion that seemed to happen at the back of Greg's shop, just as she passed it on her way home, that she almost lost her balance completely and had to clutch a tree at the edge of the pavement to prevent herself falling over. She was almost winded by the shock and stood for a moment, trembling, dazed, one hand on her chest to try to still her thumping heartbeat, the other becoming scratched, damp and begrimed from her grasping contact with the rough and mossy bark of the tree.

Whatever had happened inside Greg's shop had caused the alarm to go off and its piercing shriek rhythmically, wailingly severed the night air. She slowly and stumblingly went to the shop window on the opposite side of the door to the ET picture and peered in as hard as she could. She could see nothing except yellow, orange and red flames flickering at the back of the shop and dancing a reflection on the front window. *The window, get out of the way, you stupid woman!* she had time to think before she hurled herself forwards along the pavement and landed face down, scarf held over her head and hands as the window exploded behind and beside her. Splinters of shattered glass blew everywhere; she heard cars braking, people screaming, dogs barking, a nearby street light bulb bursting.

Slowly heaving herself up, she screamed to someone who'd stopped their car nearby and got out, to call the emergency services, covered most of her face as best she could with the scarf and went closer to the door to get a better view. It was hard to make anything out except the leaping, dancing flames inside the shop.

Then she saw Chrissy, prone and bent out of shape in front of the bikes on the right-hand side. She looked back and shouted at the passing motorist again that someone was inside.

Maureen looked despairingly at the many jagged ends of glass protruding from the broken window frame. *If I get hurt too, I'll be of no use to anyone. I can't possibly get in that way,* she thought, desperately racking her brains while her eyes flew all over the shopfront. They returned to the window. She had an idea. What the gap left by the shattered glass did allow her to do was lean forward just far enough into the shop to scan the inside of the door and notice, with a gasp, the key resting in its lock. Just to be sure, she frantically but fruitlessly grabbed the outside handle, pumping it up and down so hard that the whole door shuddered on its hinges. *Oh, what the hell!* she thought as she shakily wound the scarf as tightly as she could over her coat round her elbow, using the padded joint, harder and harder and more and more painfully, as she stood with her back to the door, to smash the window in it. She then reached in, tentatively, to turn the key, not without difficulty nor danger of dropping it on the floor due to her shaking fingers, and so unlock the door from the other side.

Inside the shop, the noise of the pulsating alarm was ear-splittingly insistent, for a nano second disorientating, but Maureen was glad of it as it brought her to her senses, quickened reactions and increased the urgency of getting out as soon as humanly possible. A vague memory from a disaster film flashed across her mind and she dropped to her knees. Even here, the smoke was thickening, swirling, catching like a blade at the back of her throat and making her retch, her eyes water. She wrenched the scarf from her arm and tied it quickly round her nose and mouth, knotting it with shaking hands at the back of her head. She peered again through the smoke, eyes streaming, to reorientate herself as to where Chrissy was. There. She slithered on elbows, stomach, knees and toes as best she could until she reached her. It was only then that she thought about how she was going to get her out. *Where the hell is her chair?*

Maureen confusedly and despairingly looked about her, gasping in air as best she could through the scarf, though every breath was scorched and painful. She saw it at last, buckled and twisted against the side of the counter. Useless. How on earth was she going to be able to do this? She looked at Chrissy, her face pale but sweating, her arms crooked and spread from the force of the blast, her legs doubled underneath her.

Maureen froze for a second and looked about her again, panicked, for some kind of solution, struggling to see anything at all clearly due to the thickening, black smoke slowly oozing from back to front of the shop. She covered her face with her hands, prone as she was on the ground. The only reasonable method that occurred to her for transporting Chrissy out of the, now almost flaming, shop in the absence of her chair was a wheelbarrow, which she didn't even know if Greg possessed. And, if he did own one, it would most likely be in the back of the shop or even beyond that in the space outside, both of which were completely inaccessible through the flames.

For a few moments Maureen lay sobbing, silently, into her hands, her whole body shaking against the hard floor. Still snuffling quietly, she then crawled to Chrissy's head, twisted herself awkwardly over and leant herself back against the bikes, lifting and putting Chrissy's head tenderly into her lap. Her face was aflame from the heat and the tears, and she could feel the fabric of her clothes starting to tear at her skin from the increasing heat.

Still quietly sobbing while stroking Chrissy's face, amid fragmented memories of Crete and thoughts of her children and grandchildren, she saw Frank's face: open, honest, loving, earnestly helpful for the competition. Competition? What on earth does that matter now as she'll never know the outcome?

She must have passed out for a few seconds because she jumped and gave a muffled scream when something shook her shoulder and an alien's face appeared a few centimetres in front of hers. Not an alien, it was Ellie, with her bicycle helmet on the wrong way round, covering her nose and mouth rather than the back of her head. Above it, her forehead was beady with sweat and her eyes blazed urgency at Maureen while continuing to shake her, so hard that it hurt. She was shouting through the cycle helmet, over the noise of the alarm, rising flames, exploding bottles, crashing debris and splintering wood and plaster, but the voice still sounded as though it was coming from a long way off. Slowly, Maureen focused.

"We have to get her out of here, Maureen. Maureen, please, I need you to help me! I can't do this on my own!"

Ellie gently picked up Chrissy's head from Maureen's lap and carefully slipped her arms under her shoulders so she could grip her hands together tightly across Chrissy's chest.

"Hurry, Maureen, get her feet. I'll go first, towards the door. Come on!"

Maureen staggered to her feet unsteadily, holding onto the bike stand then the wall so as not to fall, silently muttering to pull herself together and get on with it.

She nodded silently to Ellie, bent down and picked up Chrissy's legs under the knees. Thank goodness she was wearing trousers as it made the grip easier. Together they staggered towards the door, keeping as low as possible and trying not to look at anything except Chrissy's body and where they were treading. They had to dodge broken glass, scattered tins, debris that had once been shelves and furniture, Maureen gesticulating to Ellie with her head to help guide her round obstacles as she reversed, slowly, towards the door. Their necks, backs and legs strained with the effort: Chrissy was small, thankfully, but the heat from the fire and the exertion in warm clothes was almost overwhelming and both women panted and sweated profusely. The smell of burning rubber became almost as nauseating as the choking smoke from the fire licking the air behind Maureen's back.

As they neared the door, they could feel fresh air through the broken glass, and this gave them new impetus. They could also hear sirens, even above the unceasing, relentless wail of the alarm, so the fire engines must be close. They had to put Chrissy down to open the door, which had warped in its frame and stuck tight since Ellie's entrance. It was too dangerous, because of the broken glass, and difficult, because of the height, to get her out through the window, even between the two of them. Despite Maureen fiercely shaking her head at her, Ellie took a quick look around the frame and assessed the effort, then immediately returned to her to start kicking at the door, motioning to Maureen to do likewise. After a while, due to their frantic and exhausting combined efforts, it started to splinter and they then simultaneously ran at it with their left shoulders as they'd seen police officers do in films. It was a lot more difficult, and painful, than it looked there though, or maybe the door was just older and thicker. Eventually, it gave way and they both nearly landed on the pavement, to the astonishment and incredulity of a small crowd of people that had gathered at a distance. They immediately returned to get Chrissy and dragged her out, people running to their aid when they realised what was happening.

Two ambulances had arrived first, and paramedics immediately stretchered Chrissy into one while another medic ushered Maureen and Ellie into the other to be checked over and given oxygen. Before she could reach it, Frank was beside Maureen, gently touching her arm for fear of hurting her. Maureen looked sideways and immediately fell into his arms, not caring about the pain this caused to what felt like every muscle in her body, not to mention her hot and tightened skin.

"Thank God! I thought I'd lost you then, love." Frank was actually crying, tears streaming down his lined and reddened face. Maureen choked too, not from the smoke.

"I thought you had too, Frank."

Billy and Harry came running up too, anxious for Chrissy and Ellie. They'd been in the pub, having a few drinks to celebrate Harry's homecoming, when they'd heard the blast and commotion outside. Most of the punters were now in the crowd. Billy was pale with concern for Chrissy, worrying about having to tell her dad what had happened.

"Will she be okay, do you know, Ellie? And how about you? I can't believe you managed to get her out between the two of you."

"I don't, sorry, but they're looking at her now. She's in good hands. We'll just have to wait and see. I'm fine. I can't quite believe we did it either."

Maureen and Ellie looked at each other and managed feeble, crooked smiles.

# 32

Chrissy was okay, apart from severe smoke inhalation, some cracked ribs, some minor fractures in her arms and concussion. She had been lucky, the fire officers and doctors said. If the fire hadn't started in the rear of the shop, even Maureen would probably not have got there in time. Greg, Maureen and Ellie visited Chrissy in hospital several times, the women telling her what had happened, as gently as they could, as she couldn't remember anything after leaving her own shop. Maureen brought her homemade cake and biscuits and mothered her in a way she'd never done with her own children. Greg was devastated on Chrissy's behalf, feeling responsible for what had happened because he'd only been thinking of himself, but Chrissy, Maureen and Ellie reassured him, saying the only guilty person here was Gary.

Maureen and Ellie were told they were very lucky too. Maureen had quite severe smoke inhalation and skin irritation from the heat; she was told that just a few minutes more inside would have resulted in severe burns, probably to her whole body. Ellie escaped more or less unscathed.

Chrissy learnt over a long period of time, because the hospital staff wouldn't let the police near her at first and, in any case, she couldn't speak without pain for some weeks, that Gary had used her to get access to Greg's shop so he could tamper with the electric wiring to cause the fire, an act of revenge for what Gary considered Greg had done to his father and family. The female police officer who shared this with her, while Maureen sat next to her, holding her hand tightly, did so as gently and sympathetically as possible, but also in a very businesslike way. Gary had rightly guessed that the wiring in Greg's shop would be similar to Chrissy's own, as it would have been installed about the same time, there were limited companies available to do it then and the layout of the shops was almost identical. Gary had checked Chrissy's out while doing odd jobs in her shop. He'd rigged it so it wouldn't happen immediately but when the shop was closed. He'd planned and executed it carefully so no one would get hurt, even Greg. He just wanted to destroy his precious shop and livelihood. Chrissy had just been in the wrong place at the wrong time. Investigations were ongoing to validate how Gary claimed to have done it, just in case he had blindsided them, but he appeared to have interfered with the wiring behind sockets.

In a separate interview with Greg alone, the police told him that the explosion wouldn't have been so sudden and intense if the flames, fairly harmless at first, hadn't immediately come into contact with several rags soaked in a highly flammable lubricant, which Gary had stuffed into the wall cavities behind the sockets he'd interfered with. Had Greg not smelt anything while he was working in the repair area of the shop the day after the judging? Greg confessed that he hadn't spent much time there that day as he'd been too busy serving customers at the front, who'd come in after seeing the ET picture. In any case, feeling very stupid, he said he'd probably been too distracted by the anticipation of the judges' results later in the day and everything else that was going on.

The police officers also noted they'd found cans of the same lubricant tucked away outside at the back of the shop, concealed by a piece of dark tarpaulin. Greg's astonishment was obvious and intense. He'd never used flammable lubricants for bike repairs, no one had for years, and he certainly wasn't responsible for leaving those cans there, it just wouldn't be safe. At which the police officers looked at each other and confirmed they'd guessed as much. They hadn't asked Gary yet, and he hadn't volunteered the information, but it seemed likely he'd planted the cans, thinking the police or fire officers would find traces of the lubricants inside the shop, realise they were a trigger for the fire and match them to the cans outside, in order to make Greg himself look even more culpable, on top of having what looked like dangerous wiring in his shop. The two factors might even have invalidated any insurance claim Greg made.

They also told Greg it appeared Gary had rigged the wires and planted the rags and cans on the evening of the judging, while it was dark and attention was diverted elsewhere. The visit to Greg's shop was quite late in the judging agenda, yes? Even if Gary had been inside the shop while the judges and crowd were congregated at the front window, although he probably even had time to finish the job before they arrived, they'd have had no idea of it, and they certainly wouldn't see the movements of anyone in the area outside, behind the shop. The police officers looked at each other. Very cocky, pretty impressive really. Greg almost gagged, feeling sick, and buried his head in his hands on the table in front of him. One of the police officers quietly offered him water and said they were done for now.

They told Chrissy that to do the actual deed, Gary had climbed over the fences of the few shops separating Chrissy's and Greg's at the back of their gardens, after clearing the passageway and improving access at the side and back. If caught, he had a ready-made plan to be humbly and charmingly embarrassed and apologetic, but he'd been working on Chrissy's garden (which she would be able to back him up on) and was curious to know what they'd done with their outside space in order to help him get the best out of hers. He'd tried and timed it a few times, taking photos of where the CCTV cameras were outside Greg's so he could dodge them easily by quickly and silently hugging the fence and entering via a window, which he'd managed to pick open, but not so that it showed, which was away from the camera guarding the door to the outside. He'd made sure each time that his company overalls were covered up and had worn a large woollen hat into which he'd stuffed his striking, long, blond hair, and which he'd pulled as far down over his face as he could, just in case. He'd covered the flashlight on his phone to subdue it so he could still see where he was going but wouldn't be easily visible to anyone else.

Greg had avoided visiting Chrissy during shop opening times for fear of bumping into Greg and had always parked his van away from the high street, not wanting to advertise his presence or invite any comment or speculation. The female police officer stressed to Chrissy how Gary appeared genuinely distraught that she'd suffered because of his actions and had continually asked how she was doing during their interviews with him. A stunned, bewildered, uncomprehending Chrissy struggled to take it all in at first but eventually the truth dawned and Maureen, who had insisted on staying with her in every police interview when her dad couldn't, was there when she broke down.

The blow was lessened a little by the knowledge that Gary had been so devastated that Chrissy, even more than Greg, was the victim of his crime that he had quickly given himself up. The police told Chrissy that otherwise it could have been difficult to trace the criminal action back to him. Maureen stayed afterwards until Chrissy's dad could get there, holding and comforting her like a child.

Some time later, Chrissy asked Maureen what she would have done if Ellie hadn't arrived.

"I'd have stayed with you. There was no way I was going to leave you. I'd passed out by then anyway, so I wasn't physically capable of moving. I wouldn't have felt a thing either. But, thankfully, she did get there."

"But you didn't have to come into the shop at all. In fact, you really shouldn't have done. Even the fire officers said what you did was incredibly stupid and dangerous and they'd never ever recommend any member of the public to do that."

"Well, I did. What's done is done. Please don't worry or think about it too much. It's just another 'what if' that'll only drive you mad. I'd better go now, and let you get some rest. You look exhausted. I'll come back tomorrow, unless your dad will be here?" They hugged fiercely, silently and tearfully before Maureen left.

After leaving hospital, Chrissy went to her dad's for a month to recuperate. Debbie worked in the shop part-time to keep the business ticking over, and more people than ever came in, to find out how Chrissy was doing as much as to make Christmas purchases. When Chrissy left hospital, she did so with the mobile number of a male nurse who had helped to look after her. She'd told him that she didn't know if she would ever call him, and he replied that he'd be seriously disappointed if she didn't but didn't care how long he had to wait.

Billy won the window display competition and Chrissy was runner-up. Maureen phoned them both to congratulate them, apologising that she couldn't do so in person, sent flowers to Chrissy with a "coals to Newcastle" comment and commanded Frank to carry a bottle of single malt up the road to Billy during a break in helping in her shop with Cecily, in Maureen's absence while she recuperated. For a few weeks after the fire she considered, and talked to Frank about, giving it up. It just didn't seem that important anymore. Frank said he'd support her in any decision she finally made but suggested she give it a month or two before doing so as she was probably still traumatised, and a decision made in that state could be one she later regretted. She was glad she followed his advice. After the excitement of Christmas and the aftermath of her bravery, for which it was rumoured she and Ellie would be put forward for some kind of an award, the dullness of January set in and she was glad to have the reassuring routine of opening and attending to the shop. She became something of a local celebrity, which encouraged more people, including some who had travelled far after hearing what had happened, to come in to meet her. How could she disappoint them by not being there?

Ellie, also something of a celebrity, was offered, and accepted, a part-time job in Billy's toy shop, as soon as she felt well enough to start. He planned to use the prize money to extend at the back and would need more staff. He couldn't rely on Andy forever as he would leave school and go away to college. Harry would be home to plan, organise and project manage the building work.

The awards ceremony, which Sylvia judiciously delayed by two weeks for Maureen's and Ellie's benefit, was necessarily subdued, with Chrissy absent in hospital. Her dad and Debbie received the runner-up award on her behalf, a smaller sum of cash. Debbie hadn't wanted to, feeling at least partly responsible for what had happened to Chrissy because she had joined the online dating agency at her own recommendation, but Chrissy and her dad insisted. She was running the shop, temporarily, it had to be her. And it was important as she was a wheelchair user. She accepted the award in the same council office room where they'd held the introductory meeting, before Billy received his, with Harry and Susan by his side, Chrissy's dad's arm comfortingly on her shoulder, while she tried not to cry.

It took several months for Greg's shop to be put right. His insurance covered the use of temporary premises, so he rented a nearby business unit and set up there, as best he could, his mum and dad coming down every day for two months to help him. After Lola's exams were over, the two of them took two weeks off and went to Turkey, where she had extended family. They'd announced their relationship at the meal with her family on the evening of the fire. Lola's parents were delighted, and not entirely taken by surprise, and Berk gave Greg a mighty slap on the back that nearly made him choke. He secretly hoped that this would mean Lola would live locally to practise medicine, once qualified, rather than move away as she'd been talking of doing. Lola's brothers and their families were also welcoming. Greg was invited to their Christmas meal but had to decline as he was going to his grandparents' place with Mum and Dad.

Without condoning what Gizza had very nearly done to Chrissy, Maureen, Ellie and him, Greg did stand up for him and write a statement about what he must have gone through with his parents. The fact that he'd owned up immediately also counted for something with the judge and jury at the trial (although the judge was severe in his condemnation of Gary as, despite all his best efforts, the shop could have been full of people when the fire took hold), and his sentence was reduced as a result. Greg visited him, just once, in prison, and told him to make the best of it, as he'd done. "Learn another trade. You can hardly continue as an electrician now. And make the most of the mental health support they give. It can be really helpful. Good luck." Against his better judgement, Greg couldn't help but feel sorry for Gizza, who cried when he left, desperate for reassurance that Chrissy was going to be okay.

Early the following year, Fran and Beth got married in the council building, in the same room the initial and final competition meetings had been held. They'd admired it at the time and talked in whispers about its potential. They invited all the shop holders and their families, as well as their own families and friends. The room was decorated with banners, balloons, ribbons and flowers from Chrissy's shop. They were particularly attentive towards Maureen, who was still recovering from her injuries.

Sylvia attended a meeting with Councillor Blakeney on the Friday following the judging. She was fired up, printed evidence of his perfidy in hand. She'd dressed carefully, professionally, and even put heels on, to increase her height as well as confidence. She'd dealt very successfully with several, much more important people than him over the last few months, after all. She marched, heels clicking, into his office after knocking smartly on the door and before even being asked to enter. Jim Blakeney had his back towards her and was looking out of the window, which made her hesitate, slightly, before sitting on the seat in front of his desk. He wandered slowly, apparently pondering, over to the cabinets against the wall and tenderly touched the leaves of the nearest plant. Then he turned towards Sylvia and smiled at her.

"I'm not sure exactly why you called this meeting, Sylvia, but I feel I have to share something with you first. I'm sorry if this will shock you – it was a huge blow to all of us – but I must tell you that my mother is dying. She doesn't have long. I'm going to take a sabbatical and we're going to go and live near her until the end. I don't know how long it will be, but it's unfair to keep you in suspense. There will be a temporary replacement for me."

He gently fingered the leaves of the plant again and bent down, reverently, to smell them.

"But, regardless of that, we want to promote you. You've done excellent work on the shop window display competition. No one could have done better. I've had excellent reports from everyone involved, in particular the shop holders, who've had an uplift in profits off the back of it, which is exactly what we wanted. And didn't you go and visit that girl in hospital who was hurt in the fire? That is wonderful PR, well done. We've been looking for someone to replace you in your current role, not that that can be done, exactly."

He paused, collecting his thoughts, still lightly fingering the plant.

"What decided it was when I came back from visiting my mother, when we were told the awful news, and found these plants in my office. Even before I'd had a chance to share it with you. It was such a wonderful surprise, and they give off a healing vibe, don't you think? Can you believe it, I've even been talking to them?"

Jim Blakeney stopped abruptly and turned away from Sylvia towards the window. She could see he was close to tears. For the first time in her life, Sylvia was lost for words for at least a minute. She stood up slowly, trod softly and silently across the floor between them on her toes and laid her hand gently on his sleeve.

"I'm so, so sorry about your mother. You can rely on me. I'll do anything I can to help you and the council."

Choking a little, with awkwardness and embarrassment as well as emotion as she felt Jim's arm shaking beneath her hand, she continued, "Thank you so much for the promotion. I'll do my best to deserve it. I really am grateful. I wish you well and hope that your mother doesn't suffer too much." Sylvia turned slowly and left the office as quietly as she could, glancing briefly and guiltily at the drawer of his desk, containing the infamous bunch of keys, returned to her desk and called all of Jim's appointments for the rest of the day to postpone them.

A few days after Ellie started work at the toy shop, she and Harry celebrated with a Chinese takeaway and bottle of wine at her house. Over the meal, they talked about Ellie visiting Harry in Oman before he came home permanently and were cosied up on the sofa later, watched by a baleful-looking Alex, when she got an unexpected call from Simon.

"Mum, you'll never believe it, Jo's pregnant! We've been trying for ages, though I didn't like to say. The baby's due in six months. Everything's fine. Will you help us look after him or her? And, by the way, if it's a girl, we'd like Ellie to be her middle name."

Ellie immediately sat bolt upright, hastily rearranging her clothes. "Congratulations, Si and Jo, that's wonderful news. I'm really pleased for you. I'll do what I can to help, of course, but I've just started a new job, and," looking down at Harry, "I've got a new man. I think you might have to make other plans about regular childcare. I hope everything goes okay. I'll call you back tomorrow. I'm a bit busy at the moment. Love to Jo and hope she's keeping well. Speak soon. Bye!" And Ellie dropped the phone onto the floor beside a fleeing Alex and launched herself onto Harry, laughing.

## THE END